SILVER FOX'S SECRET BABY

CALLIE STEVENS

ONE
HARLEY

"Couldn't we have just stuck with watermelon slices?" I groan, scooping the melon baller into the honeydew for the umpteenth time. My forearm is starting to burn. "I mean, who eats honeydew anyway?"

"You'll thank me when you see how nice it looks," Gillian says with a serene smile from across the kitchen island. She's currently arranging a charcuterie board around a bowl of hummus in which the droopy, bell sleeve of her boho maxi dress is dangerously close to getting dipped.

I roll my eyes. "Next year, we should get this party catered."

Dana's ears perk up. "Why, when we have ten perfectly good hands between us?"

"Eleven!" Stella adds, holding up her two hands and grinning. Gillian's daughter is five years old and the brightest light in all our lives. Right now, she's sitting on the counter, making sure her aunt Kira is properly placing the strawberries on the flag cake. Kira doesn't say much, but her attention to detail is impeccable.

Amy laughs, "Twelve, honey. Unless you only have one hand."

My adorable niece flips her palms around and looks at them before confidently announcing, "Twelve!"

"We're working on the counting thing," Gillian says with a sigh.

"See?" Dana says to me with a jerk of her thumb toward Stella. "Twelve."

I snort in laughter. "Fine. Whatever."

"You're not getting out of this, Harley. Ever," Dana says, patting my back.

My four sisters and I are currently preparing the festivities for the annual Solace family Fourth of July party. Our parents hosted this party even before any of us were born. I guess it's only right we take up the family tradition. When times seem to be changing so fast, it's nice that some things stay the same.

And with my sisters and me at the helm, these shindigs go off without a hitch. We're the best quintet you could dream up.

"Hey, girls–" Dad sticks his head into the kitchen. "Could I get one of you to be my grill assistant?"

I scan my sisters, all of whom are silent. It's a dirty job, but someone's gotta do it. And it won't be me. I touch my nose as fast as possible. "Nose goes!"

As quick as lightning, Dana and Amy's hands shoot up to their noses, followed by Kira's more methodical motion, leaving Gillian as the loser. She looks around, despondent. "No, I can't!"

"Relax, Gilly. You don't have to touch the meat," Dad tries to talk her down.

"It's the principle of it, Daddy! I can't have any part in

it," she says, holding up her hands as if that somehow cancels out her obligation.

"But you lost 'nose goes'," I say with a smirk.

Gillian shoots me a look, lasers in her eyes. "*You* should go since you're so tired of working on the melon."

"Oh no, I've just gotten into a groove," I say, returning the melon baller to the melon.

She huffs, "You're so immature, Harley."

"I'll help you, Grandpa!" Stella pipes up and starts to wriggle off the counter.

"You know, sweetheart, while I'd love your help, this is kind of a grown-up job. Although from the looks of it, I don't see any here," he says with a cheeky smile.

Gillian crosses her arms. "I'm not doing it."

"I'll do it," Kira finally announces. "Amy, finish the cake. Stella knows what to do."

"Thank you, Kira," Dad says with a sigh. He gives the rest of us an admonishing look. "When did it become such a burden to help out your old dad, huh?"

"Dad, you know it's not that. We just...aren't the grilling types," Amy says, trying to lessen the blow with a sweet smile.

He sighs. "Why did I only have girls?"

We all laugh as Kira and Dad head out into the backyard to start the grilling.

Dad wouldn't know what to do with boys and that's a fact. He's the best girl dad there is and has set the standard high for men. Which is why none of us are married or even in a relationship. A good man is hard to come by.

A good relationship, though? I think it's probably impossible. I thought Mom and Dad were the textbook definition of a perfect couple. And then...everything fell apart. That trauma of seeing a good relationship sour has turned me into a heretic of love.

Well, that and life. I left the US to get away from my problems. Turns out that no matter where you go, problems happen, so now I'm back.

Sometimes, I just find it easier to believe that love isn't real. It's just a fairy tale made up by people who are living in blissful ignorance.

That doesn't mean that I don't still want to try and find a love that really is as deep as I thought my parents' relationship was. That's the fucked-up thing about life. You can know something is bad for you and still want it. Like alcohol or cigarettes. Love is the exact same thing in my eyes.

I try to go back to the last of the melon, but I can feel Gillian glaring at me. "Have something to say, Gilly?"

She huffs. "No."

"Gillian..." Dana says warningly.

"Just wonder if you'll ever grow up," Gillian says at half-volume.

I scoff, "Gilly, get that stick out of your–"

"Harley!" Amy interrupts, eyes wide in alarm. She bobs her head toward Stella. "Tender ears..."

I look at sweet little Stella, a near carbon copy of Gillian. "Honey, could you do me a favor and start watching for cars to pull up in the front?"

"A job?!" Stella asks excitedly.

I go over to her and help her down from the counter. "An *important* job."

"Like on your show!"

"Exactly. Now–" I say as I hustle her out of the room. "Go wait at the window and the second you see a car pull up, run your little butt in here and cry out, 'Someone's here!'"

Stella doesn't get another word in edgewise before I've shooed her out the door. As soon as it's closed, I turn back to my sisters and pick up where I left off. "Okay, *now* I can say what I really mean, which is, Gillian, get that stick out of your–"

"You seriously kicked my daughter out of the room so that you could swear? Really mature, Harley," Gillian snaps.

"You want to talk about maturity? You can't even look at a rack of ribs without breaking out into hysterics," I reply.

She clenches her fists at her sides. I love riling Gillian up. Just the little sister in me, I guess. She's such an easy target. And, it's totally counter to her "peace and love" attitude. "If you knew half of what I did about the meat industry, you would–"

"I know plenty!"

"Just because you've *talked* to a butcher on your podcast one time–"

"It's not a podcast! It's a radio show!" I host a radio show five days a week on the public radio station called *Someone's Gotta Do It*. Each week, I pick an occupation to demystify to my listeners. I've covered so many jobs from baristas to oil barons, crossword creators to cowhands, nephrologists to nail technicians. And, yes, a butcher.

Gillian lets out a high-pitched grunt. "Ugh! Whatever!"

"Need I remind you about the pamphlets on animal cruelty you passed around the dinner table when I was *literally* nine years old and the 'meat is murder' shirt you wore for three months straight until Mom made you throw it out?"

"Okay, that's *enough*," Dana says firmly, stepping in front of me. "Okay, Harley? That's enough."

I take a deep breath and cross my arms over my chest.

I'm not sure if she's trying to stop us from fighting or if she's cut the conversation short because I've mentioned Mom. Both would be valid.

Dana continues, her voice measured and expression calm. No wonder she's a grief counselor. She's grace under fire embodied. "Gillian, Harley's going to be Harley. And Harley, Gillian's going to be–"

"Vegan!" Amy pipes up, forcing a nervous smile.

The three of us look over at Amy and then burst into relieved laughter.

"What? It's true," our littlest sister says with a shrug.

"No, you're right, Ames," I say and then smile at Gillian. "I'm sorry, Gilly."

Gillian sighs, "I'm sorry too."

"Hug it out," Dana instructs.

"Ugh." I hate this part.

Gillian laughs, grabs me by the arm, and pulls me into a bear hug. "You hate hugs all of a sudden, Harl?"

There's nothing sudden about it. I avoid them when I can. But I can't deny Gillian's warm, loving embrace. Regardless of what arguments we get into, we respect each other to bits. We just know how to push each other's buttons. But at the end of the day, I know we'll be okay. The bond between the Solace sisters is unlike anything else.

Suddenly, Stella bursts through the door. "Someone's here!" she squeals. "I saw a car!"

"Great job, Stella," I encourage and then look to Dana, our leader. "Well, shall we?"

Dana looks around the kitchen. "Amy, pop the cake in the fridge. Harley, clean up the scraps. And Gillian, clean the hummus off your sleeve."

Gillian looks at her arm and groans. "You're kidding me."

We all follow Dana's instructions hurriedly and then rush into the front hall to meet our first guests, excitement pulsing in the air.

Someone knocks before we can get to it.

"We're coming, we're coming!" I shake my head. "People these days. So impatient."

I get to the door first. It's the same kind of thrill as getting to push the elevator button. It's like a little treat. I may hate the prep phase and all, but I really love this part of the parties. I put my hand on the doorknob and look at my sisters. "Well, ladies, you ready?"

"Just open the door, Harley," Dana says with an air of annoyance.

I take a deep breath. Last moment of calm before the storm. *Let's do this.*

I open the door and immediately lose any sort of composure I just gained. Because staring right at me is one of the finest specimens of man I've ever seen. Blue eyes, dark hair graying at the temples, cheeks dimpling under a trimmed beard. He's so handsome I barely even notice the woman standing at his elbow.

My insides are warm and hungry for him, this tall, well-dressed drink of water.

However, my arousal immediately twists into terror when I realize I know the man in front of me. I've known him nearly my whole life.

Grant Neville. My father's best friend.

TWO
GRANT

"A barbecue?"

"Don't say that like you're surprised."

I sort through the papers on my desk, trying to find the contract I signed earlier in the day. Somehow, it's been lost in a mountain of documents. I was just beginning to make headway on the mess when Kent called.

"You know I've been having this party every year for over twenty years now."

I stop, eyes widening. "That long now? Seriously. Wow...we're..."

"Getting old?"

"Yeah, something like that." A lot like that, actually. I'm turning fifty in just under a year. Five whole decades on this planet and not much to show for it, if you ask me.

"Well, you haven't been to my Fourth of July barbecue in at least three years. Maybe more."

I can't remember the last time I attended Kent's Fourth of July barbecue. In fact, I can't even remember the last time I was at Kent's house. The past ten years have gone by in a rush since my company, Infinium, burst onto the streaming market. We've expanded exponentially in such a short time with streaming rights, original content, production studios... and I've been at the helm of all of it.

Running a Fortune 500 company doesn't allow for much downtime, as I've learned the hard way.

"It would mean a lot if you came. At least for an hour or so. How long has it been since you've seen the girls?"

"Um...a while." I haven't been the best friend over the past decade. Sure, I've been a steady support system for Kent in the wake of his divorce. Aileen leaving him was a shock to us all, especially for our old college pal, Malcolm.

I even have some PTSD from that betrayal, I'm not going to lie.

However, when it's come to Kent's daughters, I've kept myself at arm's reach. I've been around for major events. Graduations, the first birthday party of his granddaughter, sometimes birthdays. But for the most part, I stay away. It hurts a little too much.

Even though Kent's marriage didn't work out, he has five beautiful girls and a granddaughter, a huge family, full of love and spirit and hope.

I've always wanted a family. But everything involved in getting there is too messy. Too risky. Love can make you lose all common sense. I've seen the destruction it can cause.

I don't know if I'm brave enough to face something like that.

"Two years. That's how long. Not just a while, but two whole years!" Kent says. I can hear him smiling through the phone. "I don't even think you've seen Harley since she moved back from Australia."

That's true. Last time I saw Harley was her high school graduation. She was off to study audio broadcasting at the University of Swinburne in Melbourne. I never understood why she felt she had to go all the way out there when programs at USC and UCLA were just as good. Hell, even something in the continental United States!

"Please, it would mean a lot if you came by."

I sigh, "What can I bring?"

"Just Victoria."

Victoria's my younger sister by eleven years, although she feels more like my daughter in a lot of ways. I raised her through a lot of shit. Took care of her. She's my whole heart. "That depends on her shooting schedule," I say.

"It's the fourth of July! Don't tell me people need models on Independence Day!"

Victoria has been a model for the past twenty years, ever since she graduated high school. I didn't want that life for her, but she's become one of the most sought-after faces in fashion.

"Fine, you're right. I'll do my best to book her," I say wryly.

Kent laughs, "Okay. Do what you can."

"Thanks for the call, bud," I say, remembering the papers in front of me. "But I have to–"

"I know, you're busy. Always busy. Don't worry. We'll talk more when I see you Monday."

I swallow. Never feels good when other people start excusing your business. "Yeah, see you then."

We hang up and I return to the muck and mire of trying to find this contract.

Fourth of July can't come fast enough.

"You really ought to find a different plus one to these kinds of things," Victoria says as she admires her makeup in the visor mirror. Even for a backyard barbecue, she's completely done up and dressed to the nines.

I roll my eyes. "Kent is like family, Vic."

"I know that. I'm just saying," Victoria continues. She pulls her lipstick out of her purse and starts to roll it up. "You don't even try."

I focus on the road in front of me. It's been quite some time since I've been to Kent's house and the neighborhood isn't as familiar as it once was. I don't get out to Burbank as much as I used to. I'm usually in Studio City on the lot. "Don't have time to try."

"Oh, come on, Grant," Victoria says while slathering lipstick on her lips. "Stop lying to yourself."

"If I wanted to make time for it, I would," I say defensively.

"So, you're telling me you want to remain a bachelor for the rest of your life?" Victoria asks with a raised eyebrow.

Well, I certainly don't like the sound of *that*.

"You're eligible. You're still young, you're–"

"Forty-nine isn't young."

"It is for a man with money in Hollywood," she says with a smirk.

I sigh. "Okay, point taken."

"Listen, I met a girl on my last shoot. Just your type. She knows who you are and she's interested."

I spot the house toward the end of the block, the Spanish Colonial with cream stucco and red tile roof. A quintessential LA home. Kent and Aileen were smart to buy it when they did. A property like this would go for several million now.

"Here, I have a picture," Victoria announces, pulling out her phone.

I park the car. "Damn, I think we're the first people

here."

"I knew we'd be unfashionably *early*."

That's just me, I guess. Always timely. Always thinking a little too far ahead.

"Here, she's gorgeous. Her family lives back in Croatia and she's got these amazing natural lips that–"

I push her hand away as she holds the phone out to me. "I'm good."

Victoria's blue eyes fall at the corners. "Grant, please, just– "

"Not interested, Vic," I say with a solemn smile. "Come on." I pat her cheek and then climb out of the car.

As I start up the stone walkway to the front door of the Solace house, I hear Victoria's heels hurrying after me. "Grant, you haven't even seen her!"

"Don't need to. I'm not interested in dating a model."

"A Croatian model!" she says.

"Oh, a *Croatian* model?!" I ask with phony interest.

Victoria sees right through me, stops walking, and crosses her arms over her chest. "You're not funny."

I can't stand when she pouts. As her older brother, it's annoying. As someone who has cared for her the majority of her life, I want nothing more than to make her happy. "Look, Victoria–"

"You're just scared, Grant."

I shrug. "Maybe."

She laughs loudly, surprised she's hit the nail on the head. "You can't be serious!"

"You're the one who said it!"

"Yeah, because I was trying to piss you off!"

I laugh, "You're good at that."

She's not amused.

I sigh and put my arm around her shoulder. She's nearly

taller than me in her heels. But she'll always be little to me. "Look, Victoria," I begin, guiding her a bit further down the walk. "You know how things went with Mom and Dad. You don't remember how bad it was, but I do. And I just...don't want that for my life."

"Grant, that's not how things work. You're your own person."

"History has a way of repeating itself."

"*Grant.*" Victoria pulls away from me and looks me hard in the eye. "You aren't fated to be like them. And if you believe that, you're going to be alone forever."

I raise my eyebrows, shocked she's put it so bluntly.

"That's just my two cents. You don't have to listen to me," Victoria says with a shrug of her shoulders making it very clear that she thinks I *should* listen to her.

I glance at the house, only ten feet away. We can continue talking about this later. Or preferably, abandon the conversation altogether. For now, though, we have a barbecue to attend. I go up to the door and knock as I give Victoria one last look. "Behave."

"Bite me."

I smile to myself. That's my sister alright.

The door flies open, revealing...well, it's got to be one of Kent's girls. She has the hair, the eyes, the whole nine.

This must be Harley. All grown up. And all woman.

I've never felt this way from looking at one of his daughters. This... attraction to one of them.

She wears a white distressed top that's so big it slides off her tan shoulder and tiny shorts that show off her legs. I can't help but think about what she'd look like under there after I tore her clothes off.

God, what's wrong with me? I can't be having these thoughts. Not about one of Kent's daughters. It's not just that she's younger than me. Probably nearly half my age (dear God). But she's off-limits. Completely and utterly.

"Grant?" Harley speaks first. Brave girl, since I'm at a loss for words.

"H-Harley?"

"That's me!" she says with a mischievous grin.

Shake it off, Grant. It's just a feeling. It'll pass.

I force myself to grin back. I'm just one of her dad's old friends. A friendly, paternal figure. If I don't make it weird, it won't be weird. "Well, look at you! You're all grown up!" I'm not sure if I should hug her. That might be weird. So I stick my hand out for a handshake and *immediately* realize that's even weirder.

Harley eyes my hand and lets out a snorting kind of laugh so adorable it makes me want to squeeze her tight. She takes my hand. The electricity of her touch is nearly too much to bear. But with all of my willpower, I remain steady as we shake hands. "I mean, it's been like eight years, right?" Harley says, her hand leaving mine. If I could keep her hand in mine forever, I would. "I'd hope I look a little different."

"Has it really been that long?" I scratch the back of my head. "Wow. Time flies."

"Sure does."

We linger for a moment. I haven't even clocked that she's not alone until this very moment. Three of her sisters are behind her, along with her niece.

"Ahem..." Victoria clears her throat.

"Right! Sorry!" I step aside and gesture to Victoria. "You remember my sister, don't you?"

"Of course! You're in, like, every magazine," Harley says with a smile.

Victoria looks away, flushing. She's always been

humble, even at supermodel status. "Well, hopefully, you remember me from before that."

"And you remember my sisters? Plural?" Harley says, stepping aside.

"How could I forget the famous Solace brood?" I ask and immediately regret my choice of words. Sounds creepy and antiquated.

We all exchange hellos and then settle into another silence. My eyes can't help but gravitate toward Harley. Her eyes are decorated with swipes of eyeliner, catlike and tempting.

"Why don't you invite them in? Like they're our guests or something?" Gillian whispers at a volume loud enough for all of us to hear.

"*Gillian!*" Dana scolds, but immediately picks up the torch. "We're so glad you could make it, Grant. Come in and let's get you a drink."

I nod more vigorously than I'd like. "Please, that sounds wonderful."

Dana puts a hand on my arm and starts to guide me inside. I give one last glance to Harley and, to both my delight and chagrin, she's looking right back at me. Her brown eyes are sweet and sticky, just like honey. I could die in those eyes.

She breaks eye contact first, attending to Victoria. My heart falls slightly, but I know there's nothing here. Nothing but vicious, impulsive attraction. Desire. Want.

All of that is fleeting.

However, as Dana guides me inside, talking to me in a gentle, friendly voice, I can't hear a word she says. Because there is only one thing on my mind. One voice, one image, one touch.

Harley Solace.

THREE

HARLEY

From the moment Grant walked in, I haven't been able to stop looking at him. Watching him. *Studying* him.

There's something about the way he moves. With purpose and grace, but not with pride. It should elude a man of his status. After all, he *is* the CEO and founder of Infinium Entertainment, only the biggest name in television and film for the past several years.

But I've known him my whole life. Probably before that. He's been friends with my parents since they were in college. It's wrong for me to be...attracted to him.

And yet, I can't look away.

It should be easier now that the party is in full swing and the backyard is full of people. The grill is churning out hot dogs and hamburgers (and tofu dogs and bean burgers for the vegans and vegetarians that come with the territory in LA). Music is blasting, people are laughing and splashing in the pool, the sun is just starting to grow orange, anticipating its set in the west.

After the way his eyes met mine, though...for that briefest second.

Well, how can I look at anything else?

"Close your mouth. You'll catch flies," Gillian whispers, tapping my chin softly.

Oh god, have I been staring? With my jaw dropped? So much for being subtle. I close my mouth tight. "Sorry."

"I know you're bored, Harley, but at least try to look interested," she teases, bumping me with her hip.

"Yeah, I could just...die of boredom," I affirm nervously. I can still see Grant in my periphery, in the middle of a group holding a boisterous conversation. He looks so fucking good in that thin, linen suit and airy white button-down. As if he's stepped right out of a resort in Mexico. Absolutely divine.

Ignore him, Harley. I pull my attention with all of my might away from Grant and immediately clap eyes on two familiar faces emerging from the kitchen onto the back patio. "There's Lola."

Gillian grimaces. "And Axel."

"Well, don't sound too happy about it..." I tease. Lola is Gillian's best friend and has been since they were kids. They even run their vegan bakery together in Silver Lake. Axel is Lola's brother and, from the tone of her voice, Gillian's worst enemy.

"I told Lola not to bring him," my sister says.

I scoff. "She's your best friend."

"Yeah, that doesn't mean her siblings are a package deal. We don't take each other everywhere we go."

Gillian and I exchange a look.

"Okay, maybe we do sometimes..." she says, rolling her eyes.

I look back to Lola and Axel. They're both scanning the

crowd with their matching green eyes. "They're looking for you."

"Mhm," Gillian hums and sips her kombucha.

"Are you seriously going to be an asshole about this?" I ask.

Gillian glares.

"What?! Stella's playing in the treehouse with her friends," I say, gesturing over to the treehouse that's halfway up the hill behind our house, almost completely obscured by trees and greenery. We can hear the giggles of kids running, jumping, and climbing if we listen closely.

My sister crosses her arms. "You're always picking on me."

"What?! No, I'm not," I go to sip my beer but realize that it's nearly empty, just foamy backwash. "I pick on everyone."

Gillian ignores me and turns away from Lola and Axel to avoid eye contact with them. "She just doesn't respect my boundaries with him."

"What boundaries?! He's just her brother!"

She huffs.

"What's your problem with him anyway?"

Gillian hesitates and then eyes me. "He's a property developer."

"So?"

"So?! Do you know all of the natural ecosystems he has interrupted and destroyed in the name of *infrastructure?*"

I resist rolling my eyes. It's not that I don't agree with her. Erecting buildings for the sake of capital gain is not the *most* admirable job. I'm just realizing I've never had a property developer on my show. Maybe it's time. "You should be wearing your 'Hug a Tree' T-shirt today."

Gillian grunts angrily. "God, Harley. You're such a–such a–"

I laugh. She can't even say it without getting red in the face, "An asshole?"

"No! I wasn't going to say that! You're always putting words in my mouth and–"

"Girls, girls!" Suddenly, Dad wriggles in between us, a hand on each of our shoulders. "What in the world is there to fight about on a day like today?"

Gillian sniffs the air. "She's antagonizing me, Daddy."

"I'm not *antagonizing* you." I am totally antagonizing her. Just a little.

"You know how important today is for our family," he says with a soft smile. "Can we just let bygones be bygones?"

Gillian and I glare at each other. I love her to death, but goddamn, does she get on my nerves.

"Or at least...wait to fight until after all the guests are gone?"

"I can do that," I say, subtly glancing over my shoulder to spot Grant once more. God, why should I care about egging on my tree-hugging sister when I could be ogling that work of art?

Guilt shoots through my bloodstream. My dad is *right here*. I can't be looking at his best friend with hearts for eyes. At least not while he's around.

"Gilly!" Lola's sing-song voice interrupts our conversation. "I was looking for you!"

We all turn to find Lola and Axel behind us. She's wearing a big grin and he's withdrawn and placid, as usual. Not much of a personality, that one. All work and no play make Axel a dull boy.

"Hi, honey," Gillian says, abjectly ignoring Axel as she kisses Lola on the cheek.

I manage to slink away before I have to exchange any pleasantries with the sibling pair or endure any more scolding from my dad.

Fine, so I'm not the best host. I just can't do the whole, "Oh, I'm so happy to see you!" thing.

Not when I have so much on my mind.

I shake my empty beer bottle. Need another one if I'm going to get through tonight. And to my chagrin, Grant and his crew have commandeered the space around the cooler. The bright red and white box sits idly by his calf.

If I want a drink, I'm going to have to get through him first.

I take a deep breath. It won't be so bad, will it? I'm just grabbing a drink. Nothing unusual about that. Just a normal, regular thing to do.

Unfortunately, when I'm attracted to someone and all my nerves are on fire, it's hard for me to feel I don't look crazy.

I walk over to the cooler as naturally as I can, trying to avoid eye contact with anyone. But when I'm in the vicinity of Grant, his eyes immediately shoot to me. I try to ignore it, but I can't. His eyes are too powerful. They're like magnets to mine. I look up at him and smile politely. He smiles back and nods before returning to his conversation. "Existing IPs are the only way to go these days," he says, conversing with several people around him.

No words are exchanged. That's for the best, although I wish he would say something. I'm too much of a coward to.

I bend down and shuffle through the half-melted ice for another Corona. I'm right at Grant's knee. I could just lose my balance and press my face into his leg. Feel his touch if only for one more moment.

Harley, you sound like a literal crazy person. Stop it.

"There's no market for original content anymore," Grant continues.

I frown. That's a preposterous thing to say. I find a Corona, but bury it under the ice, pretending to continue my search so I can listen a little longer.

"There's too much risk involved," he goes on. "Unless it's a miniseries."

"But there's no money in a miniseries," another gentleman replies.

Grant laughs. "Exactly. It's like investing in a new car. The value immediately plummets."

I snatch my beer out of the cooler and stand up. "That's a pretty bleak outlook," I murmur with a smirk.

His eyes shoot at me, and I immediately regret saying anything. "Sorry?"

I look at Grant and then at the people around him. They're all staring at me with interest or...disdain? I'm assuming they're all in the film industry since they're engaged in a discussion about intellectual property and production. "I just mean..." I swallow. Who am I to speak on this? Sure, I'm in the entertainment world, but I'm in radio. People usually assume it's a volunteer-level position. "It's just sad. All content was original at some point. Now we have a moratorium on what's original?"

A smile creeps onto Grant's lips. "I get what you mean. And of course, there's plenty of original content out there. But working with an IP is just a slam dunk. If it's good, people are eating up the nostalgia. And if it's bad, they hate-watch it. A win either way," he says, throwing a flashy white grin to the group.

"Is that why you got into the entertainment industry? To produce content–or should I say, to *reproduce* content that's already been made?"

His eyebrows jump and the smile fades.

Someone speaks before he can, a woman with a cropped, spikey haircut dyed an unrealistic shade of orange. "Well, it's not just reproduction. Sometimes it's adaptation or–"

"I like the term 'in conversation with'," a towering man with coke bottle glasses says in a voice similar to Eeyore.

I laugh, "'In conversation with'. I like that." I hold up my hands in surrender. But I'm not surrendering.

I never surrender.

"Listen, I'm not in the film industry. Maybe I'm not one to talk. But I am a consumer. And when I tell you that these remakes and reproductions and adaptations and–" I scan the group as I speak, stopping on Grant. Not that he gives me much choice with those ocean-blue eyes. "They're getting stale. I'm bored."

The group is silent. Until Grant's mouth splits into a bewildered smile. "Really? You're bored."

"Absolutely! I don't need another version of Lord of the Rings or Harry Potter. A live-action remake of *The Lion King*. I mean, who wants that?" I look for someone to answer. They're silent. "Not me! And not my niece. She hated that movie."

Eeyore's lips droop. "I worked on that project."

I clear my throat. "Sorry. Just being honest. My point is, Hollywood is so far up its own ass that it's lost touch with reality."

"Are you saying *we*'re so far up our own asses that *we*'re out of touch with reality?" Grant asks. It's not angry. It's a challenge. His eyebrow cocks up and his eyes narrow. *Game on*, he seems to be saying.

What that game is, I'm not sure anymore. Because while my synapses are on fire, loving each and every moment of our little game, the place between my thighs is burning harder with desire. "I didn't say that exactly, but by the transitive property..."

He laughs again and this time some of his friends laugh too. I've won them over a bit. I tend to have that effect on people. "Okay, so what *do* you want?" he asks.

"I want..." For a moment, I'm not sure what to say. Because I want him. With every fiber in my being. And that desire is made even stronger knowing that I can't have him. "I want something new. New artists. New stories. Not the same old ring around the rosy. Audiences aren't dumb." I glance at the group. "I know you think they are, but they're not."

"Do you have some stories in you, Harley?" Grant asks, tilting his head to the side, considering me from every angle.

If I was brave and maybe more unhinged than I am, I'd throw myself at him and kiss him. *That* would be a story. But this is a thing that can never be. I'll dream about it tonight and then be over it. That's the way it should be. "I'm just a radio personality. But I've heard so many stories, so many amazing things in the strangest of places. You can't underestimate the value of a good story. No matter where it comes from."

He nods slowly. "I like that."

What else do you like?

I am suddenly overcome with a wave of embarrassment. "Anyway. I should...other guests," I say, gesturing to the rest of the party.

"One second–" Grant says before I step away.

My heart pounds as he reaches toward me, grabs the beer out of my hand, and twists it off with just his palm. "Jeez, you're strong."

He chuckles. "It's a twist off."

I flush from head to toe as I accept the beer from him. "Well. Thanks. Cheers."

As I walk away, I chug half the beer in one go, hoping my heartbeat will stop racing.

It doesn't.

FOUR
GRANT

I take a deep breath and stare up at the sky. It's pink and blue like a sunburnt bruise, a beautiful combination of colors. Soon, it will be total nightfall, and then, inevitably, the fireworks will start. We have a perfect view of the city's displays.

I've stayed much longer than I anticipated staying. I should have known that Kent's party would be a blast. They always have been, ever since his dorm parties back in college.

I've been talking nonstop to old friends and new, and Victoria's been having her own fun as Stella, Gillian's little girl, follows her around. She doesn't even know who Victoria is and she's gravitated toward her. Just the energy my sister gives off draws people in like moths to a flame.

Those aren't the reasons I've stuck around this late, though.

No, the list of reasons why I'm here is short and sweet. It begins and ends with Harley.

I'm ashamed to admit it, especially since she's the daughter of my best friend and she's so young. I can't even remember my twenties, at least not well, what with all the partying and late nights.

Despite both of those things, though, she's full of fire. Of life. Just the short conversation we had over the cooler about the stories stirred my manhood to an unprecedented degree. She's sharp and witty, unapologetic. *Free.*

I haven't met many women like her, especially in this town where we all have masks on all the time to impress each other.

Since that conversation, though, I can't help but notice she's kept her distance. Maybe I'm coming on too strong. Maybe she can tell that I'm not just looking at her with kind eyes but with want. The last thing I want to be is a creepy older man. And I'd hate if she said something to her dad about me. Dear god, that would be horrible. I wouldn't even know what to say if Kent brought it up to me. I'm a notoriously bad liar when it comes to him. Especially since shit hit the fan with his ex-wife. He doesn't deserve any more lies in his life.

The last I saw of her, she was getting another stern talking to from her dad after arguing with Gillian, the one who runs the vegan bakery. Those two always seem to be squabbling. That's siblings for you.

She was rolling her eyes, arms crossed over her chest, showing off a tattoo on the underside of her arm I hadn't noticed before. From far away, I couldn't make it out. I'd love to get a closer look, though. Far be it from me to be deserving of that, though. A dad's much older best friend shouldn't be asking about tattoos and meanings.

That's a recipe for closeness I can't resist.

I forced myself to look away, which I might be regretting since I can't spot her anywhere in the crowd. There must be at least fifty people here, all getting more and more sloshed by the minute.

"Glad you could make it, buddy."

I turn to find Kent at my elbow. He's giving me a fond smile, eyes a little hazy with drink. "Of course, man. I wouldn't have heard the end of it if I'd missed it."

Kent laughs hard, head thrown back. Then, he pats me on the back. "True. You would have owed me."

I've known Kent...most of my life now. We met our freshman year of college, at the tender age of eighteen. I've been there for every big step of his life. Meeting Aileen, starting his lucrative career as an entertainment lawyer, the birth of all his children...and the not-so-happy stuff too.

The least I can do is not sexualize his daughter. Too bad my body isn't listening to reason.

"I saw you got to catch up with Harley."

I freeze, frowning.

Kent chuckles. "Or should I say, she interrupted your conversation?"

I'm too stunned to speak. I had no idea he had eyes on me at all.

"Over by the cooler...?" he asks in half-bewilderment.

"Oh! Right! Yes! I mean, no, she wasn't interrupting at all. In fact, she added a necessary voice to the conversation that was lacking, what with all the industry professionals droning on and on and–" Now I'm overcompensating for the silence. "Anyway...she's turned into a fine young woman, Kent. You should be proud."

He sighs contentedly. "Isn't it crazy? Just yesterday we were all so much younger. Things were...so different." He swallows. I can tell he's trying to push away thoughts of Aileen. It happens a lot, even though it was ten years ago now. "I wish the girls could stay little forever."

My throat constricts. What's wrong with me? The entire night I've been thinking about Harley Solace not as a little girl but as a woman. Her father is my best friend. I should want to protect her as much as he does. And yet, all I've been doing is entertaining thoughts of having her in my arms, being between her legs, and...

God, I feel like I might pass out.

"But babies get older, and babies have babies, huh?" Kent says through a lopsided smile, gesturing over to where little Stella and Gillian are blowing bubbles together.

My light-headedness isn't dissipating. I need a moment alone. Away.

"I need to hit the bathroom, Kent."

"Oh, yeah, go ahead. Use the one in the house. There won't be a line there."

I glance at the pool house where indeed there seems to be a line of sorts of people waiting for the lone bathroom. "Thanks."

I scramble through the crowd as fast as I can as my heart pounds. I try to avoid being splashed by people playing a game of chicken in the pool, pass a few couples dancing to Tina Turner on the speakers, and a dad sitting on the porch with a little girl on his lap, clearly tuckered out from a sugar high. I give him a smile and he smiles back with a subtle nod before I slip inside.

I am immediately thrown off when I realize that Harley has been in the kitchen this whole time. She's standing at the sink, dabbing her shirt with a wet paper towel, cursing to herself under her breath.

I was trying to get away from thoughts of her and now she's right here in my face.

Miraculously, my whole body is calmed by her presence, and I forget about the anxiety I was experiencing just moments ago. I forget about Kent. I forget about our history. All that exists is Harley.

"Made a mess?" I ask.

Her eyes shoot up to mine, wide and surprised.

"Sorry, didn't mean to scare you," I say. "Was just coming in for the bathroom."

Harley smiles and looks down at her shirt. "Yeah, I was just eating some strawberries and got some juice on my shirt."

Damn, that sentence shouldn't be as arousing as it is.

I clock the bowl of strawberries on the counter, one of them half eaten with a big bite taken out of it. "Must be some juicy strawberries."

"Very. You want one?" she asks, nudging the bowl in my direction before continuing to work the stain out of her shirt.

I was just going to be in and out to use the bathroom, but I'm not going to say no to an invitation from Harley. I go to the bowl and take a strawberry. As soon as I bite into it, I know what she means. Juice trickles down my chin.

Can think of another thing I'd like to be trickling down my chin... "Oh, Jesus," I say, mouth full of strawberry.

Harley laughs. "Told you." She grabs a paper towel and hands it to me.

I take the towel, our eyes meeting. "Thanks."

"You're welcome," she says with a sweet, off-kilter smile.

With her shirt now clean, albeit damp, Harley returns to the bowl of strawberries. "Have as many as you like. I shouldn't eat all of them."

"Oh, come on. It's just fruit. You don't have to worry about the calories."

Harley snorts. "I'm not worried about *that*."

I'm sad to say I'm shocked. Most everyone in LA is on

some sort of diet. Counting calories or carbs, exercising like mad, juice cleanses. It's refreshing for someone to not care about that.

"I'm saving room for dessert," she says, waggling her eyebrows.

I let out a laugh from my belly. "Oh, now I understand!"

She giggles too. When our laughter dies, the kitchen is silent, just the sound of us chomping on our strawberries. I've got to think of something quick or else I'm just going to look like a creep standing here.

"So. You're back from Australia?"

She nods. "Been back for two years now."

"Jesus. And this is the first time I'm seeing you, huh?"

"Unless you caught me on a wild night off that I have blacked out from my memory, then yeah?"

I chuckle. "You're in radio, though. That's what you said."

"Yep."

"What station?"

Harley tosses her shoulder-length hair out of her face, a proud smile on her lips. "Ninety-two-point-five WQXR. Got my own show weekdays at two."

I make a mental note of that. "What do you do? The news? Pop culture?"

"Are you assuming I do pop culture just because I'm a woman, Grant?" she asks with a raised eyebrow.

I clam up, "Oh, uh, not meaning to assume, just–"

She starts to giggle, filling me with relief. And...something else I shouldn't be feeling. "I'm just giving you a hard time. No, I do a special interest piece where I interview someone of a different occupation every week."

Now this is ringing a bell. Not just because Kent has bragged to me about Harley before but because her radio show is well-acclaimed. I've just never taken the time to listen. "That's fascinating. What inspired you to do a show about that?"

"Well...everyone needs to have a job. And they're all important in the ecosystem. I don't know, I think I got kind of fed up with everyone constantly valuing some people over others. It's like how garbage men are the real heroes of our society. Growing up, you're like 'Ew, I don't want to deal with garbage' and then it turns out it's a super respectable occupation. I think every job is kind of like that."

I smile and nod. "That's...poetic."

Harley shrugs. "My goal is to broaden empathy and respect for all careers. I've been doing it for about two years now and I've got quite a cult following." She adds that last bit with a little flourish and shimmy of her shoulders.

God, she's more adorable by the second.

"I thought radio was dead," I remark wryly.

Harley takes the last strawberry and rolls her eyes. "It is." I watch her lips wrap around the bulbous fruit, tenderly and carefully before biting through the soft, juicy flesh.

Goddamn, I'd love to know how her lips feel around the head of my cock.

Easy, boy. Kent's daughter. Off-limits for sure. "Well, I know your father is very proud of you and all you've accomplished."

Her face sours.

"What?"

"Nothing. Just now you've invoked my dad and even though he's outside, he's..." She twiddles her fingers through the air. "In the room."

I laugh, "You don't want him in the room?"

Harley's lips curl into a sensual smile. "No, I kind of liked it when it was just us."

My stomach drops. Is she saying what I think she's saying? What *do* I even think she's saying? It doesn't help that the longer I look at her, the sexier she becomes. Her white, off-the-shoulder shirt falls perfectly over her frame, obscuring her round breasts and dwarfing the curves I know she's hiding under there. And her little shorts have ridden so far up her thighs I think I might faint.

"After all, it's been years since we've seen each other. Nice to catch up without...distractions," she says with a little shrug of her shoulder.

Little does she know that *she* is the ultimate distraction. The rest of the party is fading away faster each second. All that I can focus on is Harley.

It must be something primal. Biology is undeniable. But I never felt this way about her before now (thank god). In fact, I've never felt this way about any of Kent's daughters. They've all grown into beautiful young women, all of whom are as dear to me as if they were my own family. They're like the nieces I've never had.

And now there's Harley. And I want nothing more than to throw that proxy niece identifier out the window so I can have her.

Because I want her.

"That's true," I finally say with a soft nod. I glance out the kitchen windows into the yard. Everyone is starting to congregate together as the sky darkens, distracted by the thought of fireworks. I inch closer to Harley. No one is worrying about us after all. "You have to catch me up on the kind of woman you've become. After all, the last time I saw you, you were–"

"Eighteen," she cuts me off, tilting her head to the side.

I swallow. "Still. Just a kid really."

She laughs, looking down at her feet. "Well, trust me..." Then, she returns her gaze to mine, her fiery brown eyes pulsing with intensity. "I'm not a kid anymore."

My heart pounds in my chest. That's confirmation. She's feeling what I'm feeling. Harley is a woman now. A woman who is grown and independent and *knows what she wants*. From the look in her eyes and the way her body is positioned, squarely with mine, I think she might want me.

No. I *know* she wants me.

I bite on my lower lip and smile. "I can tell."

"Can you?"

"Yes."

She flutters her eyelashes coquettishly. "How?"

Oh, I have a list of things. A list I'm more than willing to divulge, but the moment I open my mouth, the kitchen door flies open and Amy, the youngest Solace girl, enters.

Harley and I bristle apart and turn our attention to Amy.

Lucky for us, Amy is on her own bent. "It's time for cake," she grumbles and goes to the fridge.

Amy is usually the bubbliest of the Solace girls, but her brightly-colored overalls can't make up for the gloom she brings into the kitchen.

Harley goes to her sister. "What's wrong, Amy?"

"Nothing."

Harley shakes her head knowingly. "It has to do with Hunter, doesn't it?"

"Oh, Hunter. A new boyfriend, Amy?"

"*No!* I'd rather *die!*" Amy shouts dramatically and then pulls a large sheet cake out of the fridge that's decorated with blueberries and strawberries to look like an American flag.

Harley gives me a sheepish smile. "Hunter Ricks just moved in next door and–"

"He's a thorn in my side! He's always blasting music while I'm trying to draw outside! His only saving grace is his daughter, Jessica, because she's adorable and the poor thing has this menace as a father." Amy sighs heavily and looks down at the cake. "I asked Hunter to wait so that Jessica could have a slice of cake, but he just took her home because she's too tired." Amy blinks, her eyes nearly welling with tears. "She's going to miss the fireworks."

That must have been the guy sitting on the porch with the little girl in his lap. Poor thing.

"Ames, it's okay. You can save a piece for her..." Harley comforts, rubbing her little sister's back.

I've already overstayed my welcome in this conversation. I cast a lingering look at Harley. Even when she's being soft for her sister, she looks absolutely divine. It feels impossible to leave her presence, but I don't want to intrude any further.

I slip out the kitchen door without another word. Amy Solace might have just saved both Harley and me from a situation we could never come back from.

And yet, I can't help but wish we hadn't been saved at all.

FIVE

HARLEY

HAVING SET UP THE DESSERT TABLE AND MADE SURE everyone has a chair or a blanket to sit on for the impending fireworks display, I need a fucking moment alone. To catch my breath. Or something.

No matter where I go, my body can feel Grant Neville. Like he's my destination on a GPS.

Our conversation in the kitchen was a close call. Amy nearly walked in on something. What, I don't know. Thank god she was all out of sorts about Hunter Ricks or else she might have thought Grant and I were standing a little too close.

I sort of wish, though, that we'd been able to continue our little...flirtation, if I can call it that. I like how he looks at me. Even the strongest of men can't resist giving someone a once-over. I could feel his eyes traveling down my body. That's only sent my brain into overdrive thinking of all the things he could do to me.

Harley, no. This is not how you end a dry spell.

Yes, it's been a while since I've had sex. That doesn't

make it okay for me to end the dry spell with just anybody. Especially *not* my dad's best friend.

I glance over at my dad. He's laughing hard at something one of his work friends has said, patting him hard on the back. He's definitely had a bit too much to drink now that he's not manning the grill and is acting silly beyond compare.

God, I love him.

He's endured so much. I could never be the one to hurt him.

I have to ignore this urge, this pull inside me. It's just a feeling. I can control it.

But of course, then my eyes find Grant's. He's at the corner of the party, leaning up against the column at the end of the porch. Alone. Sipping on a drink. His eyes glued to me.

I want to go to him.

And I can't.

Deep breath.

I abandon my post at the edge of the party and slip into the darkness, up the small hill at the edge of the property. My gut is screaming at me to go back to him. I've been impulsive before, thinking my gut was saying the right things. But I learned my lesson the hard way.

Not going down that road again.

I get to the treehouse, scramble up the ladder, and latch myself inside.

It's a shock the treehouse is still standing. The thing is rickety and splintery. But still...magical. Pillows and blankets piled up on the floor, starry lights that go on every night to create an ethereal atmosphere, and walls covered in posters of musicians my sisters and I liked when we were younger. One Direction, The Jonas Brothers, Tupac (listen, we're from California, it's in our blood).

I've always felt safe here.

After Mom left, I stayed up here for a week straight. I slept out here, wouldn't speak to anyone, except Dana, who would bring me my meals.

This place. It's a respite from how horrible the world can be. Where I can shut everything else out and just...listen to myself.

However, not long after I've climbed inside, there's a soft knock on the trap door.

"Harley? You in there?"

My stomach drops. It's him. Grant.

I crawl over to the trap door and whip it open. I nearly lose all nerve to speak when I see his face, so close to mine, peeking out through the trap door, concern emanating from his furrowed, dark brows.

"What are you doing here?" I ask.

"You left the party so suddenly, I just..." He stops and swallows. I watch his large Adam's apple bob. His neck looks like a perfect place for my lips to settle. "Just wanted to make sure you were okay."

"Did anyone see you come up here?"

"I don't think so."

I peer through the window at the front of the treehouse. Through the branches and leaves, the party remains undisturbed. Everyone is just waiting with bated breath for the fireworks. "Okay, come in. Hurry."

Grant climbs the rest of the way into the treehouse, his long, buff body looking almost comical compared to the treehouse made for little girls. As soon as he's inside, I close the trapdoor with haste and latch it behind me.

"Are you crazy?" I ask as I turn around to him.

He's on his knees, unable to stand given how low the ceiling is in here. His pants are straining at the crotch and I can see an outline of his...god, his package is huge. *This is not good.* "Well, I–"

"What if someone saw you?!" I continue. It's not anger in my voice, but fear. What if my sisters saw? What if my dad saw?

"I was just coming to check on you," Grant says softly. "You seemed...tense. Surely, no one could blame me for just trying to make sure you're alright."

I don't know if I can wade through this little crush I've developed over just the past few hours with Grant Neville. Not when he's willing to tempt me like this. "We both know that's not why you followed me." Bold of me, I know. But I'm not going to back away from it any longer, especially not when he's followed me up to the treehouse.

And we're so utterly alone.

Grant frowns, but only for a moment. Because then he smiles. A delicious, lustful smile. "You're right. That's not why I followed you."

I try to take measured breaths, but it's hard when my pulse is starting to race.

"Tell me you're not feeling anything and I'll leave you alone. We never have to talk about it ever again, we can just–"

"No," I say sternly, tightening my jaw. I'm determined. He's going to know. "I am. Feeling something. Too much."

Grant smiles, but quickly purses his lips. "I'm trying to be good, Harley. Really, I am."

"So am I."

Grant's blue eyes fall, a lock of his dark hair falling over his forehead. "It would be wrong for us to do anything."

It would be so wrong.

And that's what makes it sound *so* amazing.

I start to crawl toward him. Inch by inch, closer and closer, until my hands are resting right in front of his knees. I feel like an animal in the best way, crawling toward my prey.

"Here. Now. With your family here."

Grant isn't leaning away from me, even though I can see the anxiety on his face. He licks his lower lip.

God, he wants me.

That only makes me want him more.

"And your dad–"

I'm not going to do this for a second longer. No more back and forth.

I want him here. *Now.*

I throw my arms around his neck and kiss him hard and deep. The moment our lips connect, my body trembles with electricity.

Grant rests his hand on my waist, plying me onto his lap. How I want him to *grab* me.

I break the kiss but keep my face so close to his that I can feel the stubble of his beard on my cheeks. "Grant?"

"What?"

"Leave my dad out of this."

His breath is growing ragged, his chest rising and falling against mine. "I can do that."

"Good."

We kiss again, harder this time, our tongues caressing each other as our hands grab for anything we can touch. The tension's been building all night and there are a million things I want to do to him.

"I want to fuck you," Grant growls.

"Then fuck me."

"Here?"

"Yes."

He rakes his hands through my hair and laughs darkly. "God, you're so fucking sexy."

I laugh and dive my lips against his neck. He sighs with pleasure. It's clear he enjoys how I'm working his neck and, fuck, I'm enjoying it too.

Grant wraps his hands around my ass, fingers touching the bare skin of my thighs. "Harley Solace, you are a *woman*."

Yes, I fucking am.

I slide my hands under his jacket, pushing the sleeves down his arms. Grant chuckles through my lips, the resonance making my body buzz. In return, his hands slide under my shirt, grabbing at my bare waist. I moan against his neck and then pop my lips away, murmuring, "God, we have to be quiet."

In the distance, the popping of fireworks begins. Loud and booming.

Our eyes lock. Grant wears a sneaking smile. "Do we now?"

I nibble on my lower lip and push my hips down onto his lap. "Guess not."

Grant gasps at the feeling of my hips on his. I can feel his hard length throbbing through his pants. "Dear god, Harley..."

I start to grind my hips back and forth. "You like that?"

"Nnngh..." Grant's head dips back, teeth gritted. "Feels so fucking good."

Now that the truth has been admitted, nothing is holding me back. Not even knowing how wrong this all is.

I've never been a good girl. I've always wanted to make things a little messy.

Suddenly, Grant wraps his hand around the back of my

head and yanks my ear to his lips. "Let me fuck you like you deserve."

Grant is a powerful man. A businessman. I know the type. My dad is one. I've dated a couple. They don't like to waste their time when they know what they want.

And he's made it clear. He wants *me*.

Grant aggressively grabs the waistband of my shorts, undoing the button and zipper. He shoves them down and slips his hand around my ass cheeks, squeezing with need. I follow suit and furiously unbutton his thin shirt, each button revealing more of his broad, chiseled chest, sprinkled with salt and pepper hair.

Outside, the fireworks are growing stronger and faster. Popping has turned into booming, occasionally shaking the treehouse with force.

"What do you like, Harley?" Grant asks, pausing his actions. His words are careful, almost tender. "What do you want from me?"

I could melt right there. Young guys never ask questions. They never care what I want. They only care about how fast they can shove themselves inside me and finish the job.

Normally, I'd like him to go down on me, play with me, *arouse* me.

But this whole night, from the moment he arrived, has been foreplay.

"Grant..." I whisper in his ear. "I want you to show me what it is like to be fucked by a *man*." I jerk my hips on him hard to emphasize. "I want you to use me." Again. "I want you to *take control*."

Before I can thrust again, Grant flips me onto my back, my head resting right before the trap door. He holds me down by the wrists, eyes blazing with an animalistic intensity, jaw jutting out. He looks like he might devour me.

And I'll let him.

"I've been watching you all night," he says. He takes one finger and slips it into the waistband of my panties, pulling them down with painful slowness. "Couldn't take my eyes off of you," he whispers.

I feel his knuckle nudge against my clit and my hips buck reflexively.

Grant chuckles at my body's response. "Wanted to touch you...taste you..." He lowers his face to my neck and breathes in deeply. "*Smell* you."

Goosebumps. All over my skin.

"I don't know what you're doing to me, Harley."

I slip my free hand in between us and cup his swollen length through his pants.

"Take it out," he says gruffly.

As I undo his pants, Grant starts to trail kisses down my neck to my collarbone. The closer his lips get to my tits, the harder my nipples are getting. Before he can get there, though, I slip my hand into his briefs and feel his hot, throbbing cock with my bare hand.

"Oh my *god*..." he sighs in pleasure.

I start to run my hand up and down his length and, *my god,* is it the textbook definition of length. And width. "Need you inside, Grant."

"Guide me."

The ultimate control. Asking me to do what he can do for himself. Giving me a power that I know he could immediately revoke.

Makes me even wetter.

Wordlessly, our hips gravitate together, me guiding his

cock toward my wet center. As soon as the head dips between my folds, I lose all sense of time and place.

The world is only this treehouse and Grant. Anyone beyond it doesn't matter. It's just our bodies, slowly slipping together into oblivion.

Regret can happen later.

"Fuck, you feel amazing," he whispers as he slides further and further into me. He grabs one of my legs and bends it around his waist. "Wrap your legs around me."

He knows what he likes and he's in control. I'll do whatever he says.

Grant's neck strains as he begins to slide in and out of me, each stroke pushing his cock further and further to the hilt.

The stretch feels amazing. Like nothing I've ever felt. He's big, but it doesn't hurt. And he's hitting places inside me I never knew a man could actually hit.

He might just make me come from this.

One of his hands slides down from my wrist to my chest, pulling down the neckline of my shirt, revealing my breasts.

"Look at your perfect tits." They bounce as he thrusts inside me. "Fuck..." He cups one of them, pinching the nipple. My body seizes with unexpected pleasure. "You like that?"

I moan with a nod.

"Answer me with words," he says through clenched teeth, continuing to roll my nipple.

"Yes, I like it," I say breathlessly.

Grant puts his hand on my cheek, thumb brushing my lower lip. "Good girl."

I wrap my lips around his thumb just as I did around

the strawberries earlier. His pupils dilate further and he begins to thrust faster.

More fireworks popping and booming, echoing our pleasure. The rickety treehouse floor is starting to squeak under us.

Somehow, by fucking here, we are consecrating this place. Safe, secret, away from the world. Here, we can indulge in this illicit connection without fear.

Here, I'm not afraid of how right this feels.

I wrap my arms around his back, hooking my hands on his shoulders, forcing the tempo faster.

"You've got to be fucking kidding," he laughs into my hair.

I'm warm all over, especially in my pelvis where I'm starting to burn like molten lava. Hot, desperate pleasure. It's happened so fast. Too fast. It's almost scaring me.

Grant abruptly lifts his torso and pushes my knees together. I howl in euphoria, the space for him even tighter than before. "Let go, Harley. Let it all out."

I have no choice but *to* let it all out. Thank god the world outside the treehouse is loud and rumbling because, inside the treehouse, it's just as cacophonous. My wails, his grunts. The July heat has caused us both to sweat, made even worse by the stuffiness of the treehouse.

Just shows how hard we're working for this.

I'm starting to tremble. No rhythm to it. Just shaking. My legs, my belly, my hands. "Oh god, Grant. You're making me–I feel like I might–" This has never happened to me before, not without significant preparation or foreplay or toys or something. But here, with Grant, the elusive female orgasm isn't so elusive.

"You're almost there, baby," he murmurs. "I'm going to take you there."

Yes, he is. All the way to the edge of the cliff and then–

I scream out his name as if he might help me hold on, but it's no use. The orgasm hits me, explodes inside just the like the fireworks outside. Except, it's better.

Especially when Grant comes too. His hot seed pours inside me, adding to the overwhelming heat.

"Fuck, Harley, fuck, fuck, fuhhhh..." He trails off, his body stuttering with the final thrusts and echoes of his pleasure.

And just as we fall, the world outside is silent. The fireworks have ended. Now, our breath is loud and chaotic as we both try to get back to reality. To ourselves. Our eyes meet, Grant still buried inside me, holding the seed at my deepest part.

I fall into his deep blue eyes like I'm diving into the ocean. I cup his cheek in my hand and smile up at him. It feels like there's possibility here. A world of discovery. Of our bodies and minds. It doesn't have to end. It could–

"Harley!! Are you up there?" Dana's voice calls in the distance.

As quickly as it happened, it ends. I shove Grant off of me. "Fuck," I whisper, pulling all my clothes back on.

Grant looks like he's shaking as he tucks himself back into his pants and does up the front of his shirt.

"Shit, shit, shit, what do we do?" I ask. There's only one way out and one way in.

"You go and I'll sneak out after," he replies as if it's the easiest thing in the world.

I reach for the trap door.

"Wait–"

I feel Grant's hand on my shoulder. He tugs me back toward him. "Your hair." He combs his fingers through my hair, intense focus on his face. "There. That looks better."

As I sit there, I realize Grant Neville is the most beautiful man I've ever seen. He's always just been my dad's friend. Extended family almost. In all these years away, I haven't even paid him a thought.

What a waste of time.

"We shouldn't again," he says suddenly.

I know he's right. Yet, it stings.

"You know that, Harley. Right?"

"Yeah. Yes. I do."

Grant furrows his brow, hand resting at the nape of my neck.

"Harley?!" The trapdoor shakes. "Did you lock yourself up there?! What's going–"

Impulsively, I lean forward and kiss him. "Thanks. That was fun."

"Yeah, it was," he whispers back.

And then, I leave his embrace. I give him one last look over my shoulder before hurriedly opening the trap door and scurrying down to Dana. "Jesus, can't a girl get a moment alone around here?!" I snap.

"You missed the fireworks."

I have to hold back a laugh. "No, I didn't."

Dana frowns at me like I'm crazy. "We should...start cleaning up."

I follow her down the hillside. I still feel that gravitational pull back to the treehouse where Grant lies in wait to make his escape.

I didn't miss the fireworks. Not even a bit. I had a whole fireworks show of my own.

Too bad it'll never happen again.

LA traffic is no joke. Just as bad if not worse as people say it is. I'm running late to coffee with Kent, left too late to miss the midafternoon rush. I should have had him come up to my office in Studio City instead of me having to go down to Beverly Hills. But since everything that happened at the Fourth of July party...I'm more than happy to bend over backward for Kent.

It's the least I can do for fucking his daughter.

That's such a crude way of putting it, especially when it felt much more spiritual than that. It felt like our souls really met each other for the first time. Maybe I'm just a delusional old man, but for the first time in a while, I really felt something. Harley made me feel something.

The only upside of the traffic is that I've managed to align the trip with Harley's daily radio show. I'm ashamed to admit it but I've been listening to it every day for the past two weeks, even going through the archives on the WQXR to listen to old episodes.

I've got to say, she's an absolute pro. She manages to

somehow handle her guests with the utmost respect and is also able to probe them with questions most people might get slapped in the face for asking.

This week, she's speaking with an animal breeder. Currently, through the speakers of my car, a cross-examination is going on.

"Is there really a thing as responsible breeding?" Harley asks, her black cherry voice slinking out of the speakers. Somehow, though she's only in her twenties, her voice resonates with more wisdom and gravitas than should be allowed.

"Absolutely. As you can see from our livestreams, the conditions are immaculate. The puppies are loved from the moment they're born and are able to go into homes without histories of illness or trauma," her guest, an older woman with a crinkly voice, replies. I think her name is Marcia.

"Yes, of course, I don't mean to question your level of care," Harley responds. I can hear another question lingering in her voice. She manages to keep me hooked. And it's not just because I can't get her out of my mind. The reviews of her show say just as much as well. "But when our animal shelters and foster systems are full to the brim with animals that are in need of care, is purposefully breeding them an ethical thing to do?"

Her guest pauses.

"I'm only asking. I hope that over our past three days together, I've proven to you that all my questions are from a place of curiosity rather than judgment."

Yes, curiosity. That's a word I could use myself these days.

I'm very *curious* about Harley Solace. I've somehow managed to explore her body, get to know what she likes, the feeling of her luscious hair in my hands. But I still don't *know* her. I've never known her. Even when she was a girl. By the time she was born, I was becoming busier and busier with work. The second youngest Solace girl.

Too bad I can never be close to her again.

I finally make it to Urth Café, an LA staple. Kent loves it because they do fun art on their matcha lattes. He's a kid at heart. Maybe having so many himself keeps him young.

The moment I clap eyes on him, my heart sinks. He's sitting at a café table on the sidewalk wearing a pair of aviators. He's a generally good-looking guy. I'm not sure why he hasn't tried dating since his divorce or what he's waiting for. His excuse is that he looks too old, but I think his graying dirty blonde hair and wrinkles appearing on his forehead just make him look more...refined.

What do I know, though? I'm not a woman.

"Hey! Over here!" Kent shouts, raising his hand when he spots me. His grin is so dopey I feel like a monster. I haven't seen him since the party, haven't had to face my guilt right in the eye like this.

I slept with his daughter and he doesn't even know what a horrible person I am.

It was a one-time thing, Grant. Will never happen again. A total fluke.

Yes, a total fluke. A waking dream. That means it basically didn't happen. Right?

I go over to the table. "Sorry, I'm running late."

"Don't worry about it. Got you a latte. Half-caf. I know you're trying to cut back," he says, gesturing to the cup of coffee at the empty chair. It looks like the barista made a heart design with the milk.

"How much do I owe you?" I ask as I take a seat.

Kent scoffs. "You're joking, right?"

"Maybe." Maybe not.

"It all comes out in the wash, right?" Kent says before swiping his matcha latte off the table and taking a long sip.

We've been friends long enough that the money equals out in the end, although I'm the one with the heftier bank account these days.

"Besides, what are friends for?" he adds.

Apparently, for fucking your daughter.

Jesus, this intrusive thought just isn't going to quit, is it?

"How've you been since last I saw you?" Kent asks.

"Trying to recover from my hangover," I say with a half-smile.

Kent laughs. "Did you really go that hard at the party?"

He hasn't made a double-entendre on purpose, but that's right where my mind goes. "Hey, when you have an open bar, it's hard for me to pace myself," I say, trying to remain light-hearted.

"So, you had a good time?"

A great fucking time. "I did. I've been missing out these past couple of years."

"What about Victoria? I barely got to talk with her, I'm afraid," he says sheepishly.

I swipe my hand through the air. "Don't worry about it. You know she doesn't take it personally."

"I know, but isn't it weird that I see her more on billboards and magazines than in person? Jeez, I remember when she was this high," Kent says, holding his hand up to his shoulder.

I chuckle. She used to be such a squirt. Then she turned fourteen and had a growth spurt beyond reasonable measure. "Well, we can organize a dinner when she's back in town."

"Of course. She's hard to catch."

I sip my coffee and shake my head. "Just splitting her time now between LA and New York. I get her every couple of weeks."

"You're a good brother, Grant," my friend says with a meaningful smile.

I try to smile back. I might be a good brother, but I'm a terrible friend.

"She still single?" he asks.

I gape at him. "Are *you* asking?"

"No! Oh god, no, I'd never–" Kent clutches his heart and laughs. "I'd never do that to you. Never even...never even dream of it."

I'm sure he's dreamed of it at least once, especially back when she was a Victoria's Secret Angel.

"I'm just asking. I have some new clients that I–well, I can't disclose their names of course."

"Are you trying to set my sister up with someone entangled in a lawsuit?"

Kent guffaws. "Anyone worth anything in LA is entangled in a lawsuit, Grant."

If that ain't the truth. Infinium is involved in several at all times. That's just how the game works. Everyone always wants a piece of you.

"You know, it must be hard for her to date when she's so well known, you know? I can't imagine how you could ever be sure..." Kent trails off. "Well, I guess even for normal people you can never be sure."

My heart twists in my chest. There he goes, thinking about Aileen. They had been married for almost twenty years. And then the rug was pulled out from under him by Malcolm Jenkins, a man he trusted. Someone we had known since we were eighteen.

Kent knows betrayal all too well.

And now, I'm the second friend who has betrayed him. He doesn't deserve such crappy friends. Not when he's got such a big heart.

"At least I have the girls. You know?"

Another stab. "How do you mean?"

"Well, you don't know, I guess, but having kids is committing to allowing someone to always be growing and changing and...learning." Kent sighs. "They're never perfect, but I love them. There is no way they could disappoint me."

Not like a friend could, I guess. And it makes sense. If Kent somehow found out that Harley and I had slept together, he would choose Harley. As he should. He'd see me as some sort of bad, older man. I can hear his voice now. "You should have known better. You're so much older. She's still so young, Grant."

Younger women are tempting. I've thought that each year I've gotten older. But they are *young*. Some of them are immature. Others are still trying to find themselves. They're all utterly naïve about what life is like as you get older. The last thing I'd want to do is interrupt someone's growth. And until Harley, the thought of being with someone younger had never crossed my mind.

And as I see it, one night with Harley is more than enough. That way, we can't fuck anything else up. It was just sex. We were intoxicated with beer and fireworks. It was a fluke.

A mistake.

"Anyway, enough of that," Kent says, shaking off the somber energy of the conversation and then smiling at me. "Tell me. What's been going on with you?"

I take a deep breath, pushing down every thought I've had over the past two weeks since all of them are colored with Harley.

Time to turn on the bullshit.

SEVEN
HARLEY

"Harley, where is your helmet?"

I put down the kickstand on my motorcycle and smile over my shoulder. "Calm down, Dana."

She crosses her arms, leaning against the doorframe of her little Burbank bungalow. She used to live with Dad until a few years ago when she moved into this place. Of course, she didn't go very far. Of the five of us, she's the most attentive to his needs. That's the way she's always been since Mom left, maybe because she is the oldest. "I'm not going to calm down. If you got in an accident–"

"Dana, seriously, it's ninety degrees out," I interrupt. "You should be happy I'm at least wearing a leather jacket," I say, sliding it off my arms and I come up the walkway to meet her.

She twists her lips in annoyance. "Well, you're also late."

"I know. I rode the middle of the lane all the way here. Traffic was just crazy."

"I hate when you do that too."

I slide past her into the entryway. I can hear my other

sisters already talking in the other room. "Chill out, Dana. I'm here. I'm in one piece."

"Shoes," Dana says before I can take another step into the house.

I let out a big sigh as I look at the line of shoes up against the wall. "Right." I bend over and start to unlace my boots. I started riding choppers back in Australia. My family was *not* happy when I came back with Harleys on the brain. "Harley riding a Harley? This is a family embarrassment," my dad had joked.

The wind in my hair and the freedom I get from being on a bike make up for all the gear and the leather that I have to put up with.

It just gets so fucking hot sometimes.

I unlace one boot, then the other, and just before I can walk into the other room, Dana stops me again. "Harley—"

"Jesus, Dana, what?!"

Dana raises an eyebrow. None of us can talk back to her. Not anymore.

"Sorry. Just...I'm hot. Is the AC on?'

She chuckles. "Blasting."

I rub the back of my neck, slick with sweat. "What is it?"

"At the Fourth of July party..."

My stomach drops. *Oh no.*

"When I found you in the treehouse."

Shit. Shit, shit, shit. I've been caught. I don't know how or what she knows, but I know that this secret I've been keeping for the past two weeks is about to slap me right in the face. As if thinking about Grant nonstop isn't enough, now my sister is about to reveal that the whole family knows and I'm a disgrace.

"Were you with someone?" Dana finally asks.

Okay, that could have been worse.

"N-no..."

"Harley."

"I wasn't."

"I heard a man's voice."

I examine her face, my sweet older sister who has the patience and attitude of a saint. She's genuinely asking. If she knew it had been Grant, she'd be much more admonishing. "Okay, you caught me."

"I knew it!" she beams. "Who was it?"

I shake my head. "Doesn't matter."

"Yes, it does."

"No, it really doesn't. It was a one-time thing, so it doesn't matter."

Dana watches me for a moment and then nods slowly. "Okay, you don't have to tell me."

Thank god.

"But I think you should see whoever that was again. Because you were glowing for like an hour afterward."

I gulp. "Huh?"

"You know. You just looked..." She gestures her hand over her face. "Radiant. Whoever that was really brought something out of you."

Yeah, he brought something alright.

"You deserve someone to make you happy like that."

I let out a hum of surprise. I haven't been with anyone since I returned to the States. I left behind a whole failed relationship in Australia. In fact, that's why I left the land down under. To escape. Now, back in the States, I've renounced love openly and avoided any potential dating relationship that's come my way. Not that there have been many. I'm not on the apps. That alone makes it feel like the world is a ghost town when it comes to dating. Sure, since returning I've had a few one-night stands here and there. Never the same guy twice.

That way, they can never control me.

But hearing Dana say that I glowed after having sex with Grant, that means something to me.

"Come on," she says, nodding her head toward the living room.

I grab her arm. "You haven't told any of them, have you?"

"No."

"Okay. Good. Please, let's just keep it between us."

Dana cocks her head to the side, silently asking, *Why?*

"You know, I'd never hear the end of it if they found out I desecrated the treehouse," I say. It's as good a cover as any. We both know the rest of the girls would be furious to know I'd used the treehouse for my devious delights. This is the perfect way to avoid any more scrutiny. Because the last thing I need is my sister hounding me to find who the lucky guy was.

She laughs. "Secret's safe with me, Harley. Come on."

I go into the living room and find my sisters splayed out in various states of relaxation. I join them after quick hellos, hugs, and kisses, finding a spot on the floor in front of the coffee table where there's already a can of Dr. Pepper waiting for me. I know soda isn't good for me, but I can't get enough of the stuff.

The conversation is already in full swing about Kira's upcoming twenty-eighth birthday.

"What about a camping trip?" Gillian asks, excitedly clapping her hands together.

Amy rolls her eyes and shakes her head. "There's no way you're getting me to sleep on the ground. No way, no how."

"Guys, really, I don't need a party," Kira says in her measured voice.

Usually, given that she speaks so infrequently, her word is taken as gospel. In situations like this, however, where birthdays are more of a family event than an individual one, she is immediately steamrolled by Amy's suggestion.

"How about we go to one of those stores where we can create our own lipstick? Or our own perfume?"

"Ugh, those places are all filled with chemicals," Gillian says. "No way."

Gillian, Amy, and Dana go in circles a little longer, Kira remaining silent. I glance at my older sister with a sympathetic look. She shrugs and shakes her head. We are a little less than two years apart and have an unspoken bond, almost like twins. She's the quiet, I'm the loud. She's the moon, I'm the sun. A dynamic duo.

"You guys, she said she didn't want a party," I say loudly.

They all stop and look at me. Then Dana says in a coddling voice, "Are you absolutely sure, Kir?"

"Yes. Promise. Twenty-eight isn't anything to write home about."

"It's your birthday. Every birthday is something to write home about," Gillian says with a sniff.

"You're just saying that because you have a kid," I say after a sip of Dr. Pepper.

Gillian frowns. "Exactly. Birthdays should always be special."

We go on about this for a little bit longer before the conversation moves on to more personal matters. I sort of zone out as Gillian starts to rant about her vegan bakery and how Lola is trying to get Axel to find them a new property on Melrose.

I stay quiet. Sure, I have tons of opinions, but Gillian wouldn't care much about what I have to say, anyway. Plus, after everything that happened at the Fourth of July party, I can't afford to have any of them think something is going on with me, or else anxiety might pour out of me like a sieve. Especially given how my cover was nearly blown with Dana's curiosity.

The past two weeks, I've avoided my sisters like the plague. Not to mention my dad. Looking him in the eyes is going to be absolutely impossible after what I've done.

We all experienced one of the greatest betrayals a family could experience. When Mom left, we all had to pick up the pieces together. We only knew we could trust each other. I know Dad, out of all of us, is still learning to trust again.

How horrible would it be if he learned he couldn't trust his own daughter?

Sure, it takes two to tango. I just can't help but think I should shoulder more of the guilt since I'm Dad's flesh and blood. That's the biggest kind of betrayal there is.

And yet...despite the guilt and fear of being found out, Grant Neville hasn't left my mind for more than a minute. I've replayed our encounters so many times. The banter at the cooler, the flirtation in the kitchen, the amazing sex in the treehouse.

I can't seem to shake him off, no matter how much time goes by.

I'm screwed, aren't I?

It's not easy to be the outspoken sister. Because my silence is somehow very loud to everyone. When I'm not offering my opinion or making a quip at someone else's expense, people immediately think something is wrong.

Usually, they're right.

"Earth to Harley!"

My eyes snap to Amy who is waving at me from across the room.

"You okay? You got all glassy-eyed there."

"Are we boring you?" Gillian asks with a scowl.

I try not to glare at my older sister. "No...just thinking."

"Just zoning out, as per usual," Gillian mumbles.

I do have a tendency to do that. I'm usually thinking about my next story, my next move.

Not my dad's best friend.

I don't want to bring any more attention to my distraction. Moving right past my sister's rudeness, I ask, "What are we talking about?"

"Boys," Amy says with a tiny shrug.

Boys. As if we're still kids staying up past our bedtime chatting about our crushes. I don't do the crush thing anymore. I do the intense one-time, life-altering sex in tree-houses *thing.*

"And we've just landed on the subject of," Amy smiles devilishly, "Dana and Drewwwww."

Dana rolls her eyes. "Stop. No."

"Come on, just your names together are cute!" Amy giggles.

Drew was Dana's patient up until a few months ago. Now, the two of them have become fast friends. Based on his eagerness, we've all assumed it might be a little more than that. "Has he finally asked you out?" I ask.

"No! And he never will because *we are—*"

Kira interrupts in her usual, serious way, "You keep saying you're just friends, but from how much you talk about him—"

Dana's eyes widen. "It's taken me months to feel like

I'm not breaking the code of ethics by getting coffee with him. *Dating* him would be–"

"You've been thinking about it, though," Kira adds with a subtle smile.

Dana grunts frustratedly, gripping the couch cushion. "I'm done talking about this. Drop it."

The rest of us exchange glances. Dana is the only one of us who gets the privilege of demanding we leave her alone. She's gotten the shit end of the stick so many times being the eldest. Now that we're all grown and can recognize everything we've been through together, we give her as much space and respect as she asks.

Even though I'm desperate to hear about what's been happening with her and Drew.

Gillian claps her hands together. "Well, anyone else have any movement on the dating front?" She starts to scan our faces for a response.

The room is silent.

I feel my cheek start to twitch. Or is it my imagination? I obviously don't have anything to share, certainly not on the dating front. Grant and I had sex. That's not romance whatsoever. And yet, I'm thinking about him all the time, wondering if he's thinking of me. More dangerously, I wonder if what happened between us can ever happen again.

Gillian can't see all that on my face, can she?

She sighs. "Well, we're pathetic, aren't we?" Gillian says drolly, leaning her head in her hand.

The rest of us burst out laughing. For five sisters in their twenties to all be single is definitely out of the ordinary in most people's eyes. But we're all in this shit together.

We always have been.

EIGHT
GRANT

"*ABEL RIVER* WAS A HALLMARK OF A WHOLE generation. A reboot right now would hit right upon the nostalgia that people have for the nineties and introduce Gen Z to the IP, which would give it a whole new life."

I hold back a sigh. I've been told my sighs translate even louder over the phone. I glance out the window of my office down into one of the lots where some people are carting set pieces into soundstage C. "*Abel River*, huh?"

"I've already spoken with Tina Tharman about reprising her role and she's *in*," the man on the end of the phone, I've forgotten his name, is pitching himself to be the showrunner of...another reboot.

Ever since my conversation with Harley at the Fourth of July party, her blatant disapproval of reused stories has been at the front of my mind.

Hell, Harley has been front of mind since then too. Half the time when I'm talking with people, I completely lose the thread of the conversation remembering all the things she did to my body and the way her hands –

"I've storyboarded the whole first season," the man

interrupts my thoughts. "I know we can squeeze at least three out before general interest goes down. And who knows, it could be hit material."

Is this why I got into entertainment? To guess how long people will hold onto the nostalgia for old intellectual properties before they lose interest and we stop making money? That's...sad.

I started Infinium because I love stories. Not the stories of my own life. Those could stand to be better. But humans need stories. They need escape. Action movies to make us feel like heroes, romances to make us feel like lovers, philosophical mumbo jumbo to make us feel like we might have brain cells that haven't melted from staring at screens. A good story reaches right into your soul and stirs it up.

All the work Infinium produces now, though, is bullshit.

I know I have a hit by how loud my bullshit meter goes off.

It's sad, isn't it?

"We can even work on making it 'woke'," the showrunner says. I can hear the air quotes. "Get a consultant for things like that."

Now, I sigh. Can't help it. White showrunners really think they can catch up with modern standards of creation by hiring someone to do the work for them. "*Abel River*, huh?" I lean on the windowsill and rest my head on the glass. "Sure. Why not." I'm going to regret a flippant yes. But my mind is bouncing all around, in five different places at once.

"Really?" the man's voice nearly squeaks. "I mean—wow, I thought—"

"Send the documents over to my assistant. We'll get an in-person meeting in the books. I want to see your storyboard. And I want a few more people attached to the project before we move forward. Get something in writing from Tina Tharman."

"G-got it. Got it," the showrunner replies hurriedly and then rattles off a slew of thanks yous before I politely say goodbye and hang up.

The moment I pull the phone away from my ear and am left in the silence of my office, my body completely relaxes.

This has been the norm lately. I'm not present for the work I do like I was only three weeks ago. Now, my head is always split in half. One part focused on where I need to be, and the other part always flushed with thoughts of Harley Solace.

I thought time would alleviate my desire for her, but it hasn't. The ache inside me remains. My body yearns for her at all hours of the day. Is this a curse for betraying my friend? Am I going to be cursed with desiring Harley for all of eternity, with never being sated by the thought of another woman?

Perhaps in the scheme of things it hasn't really been that long. But I'm nearly fifty years old. I don't have the excuse of youth and immaturity. I've been around the block and seen a lot.

A young woman shouldn't completely throw my world off its axis.

And yet, Harley has.

A knock at the door interrupts my thoughts. Pity, I wanted to revel in self-loathing a bit longer. "Come in!"

The door flies open and in comes my head of PR, Resa Blackwell. She's got her thick black hair piled on her head like a beehive and her black-framed glasses dwarf her face. "Do you mind if we start our meeting early today, Grant?"

"Not at all."

Resa buzzes in, followed by her assistants, Carlyle and

Kim, both of whom started as interns at USC and now have full-time positions on the PR team. I sometimes mix them up. They have the same generic long, bleach-blonde hair, carry the same luxury purses, and drink the same colored smoothies. They're quintessential California.

The four of us settle into the seating area, the three of them clumped together on the long leather sofa and I settled back into a dark blue wing chair.

"First thing's first, we need to address how we are going to deal with the nightmare that is Flick Harrison."

I run my hands over my face. "Right, yes. Of course."

Flick Harrison, star of one of our most lucrative shows, has just been embroiled in a humongous scandal that includes an affair, tax evasion, and illegal street racing.

"We've already addressed our audiences with our original statement, but now we have to start massaging out the details of keeping Flick on the show as long as he doesn't have to serve any time," Resa explains. "Everyone likes to play morality police nowadays and forgets that pretty much every actor in the fifties was an adulterer with a second family," she says with a burbling laugh.

I love Resa because she makes situations like this feel like tiny sparks rather than fires. It's just what happens when you run an entertainment conglomerate. Things are constantly going to shit.

"Now, I've put an embargo on Flick doing any press. And I know his lawyers are instructing him to do the same," Resa continues. "But our audiences are starting to get antsy. We need to spotlight the rest of our talent and programming. And while marketing is doing a great job on that, we need to come up with some more community-based ways to get audiences reengaged with us."

"And not in an internet troll way," Kim says with a twist of her lips.

"Right..." I trail off, leaning back in my chair and hardening my brow.

"We want to give people a peek behind the curtain of Infinium. Make them feel like they know us better and know what we stand for," Resa says. "Without letting them know what's really going on behind the scenes."

"So, pop-ups, community events, interviews–" Carlyle begins to rattle off.

Interviews. I don't know if it's just because my mind is in the gutter or if it's a genuinely good idea, but an interview on Harley's show sounds like a phenomenal idea. "Public radio," I say abruptly.

The three women all look at me like I've just grown a second head.

"Like NPR?" Kim asks as if NPR is a curse word.

I laugh. "Something like that. Listen–" The more I think about it, the more brilliant I feel. "A friend of mine, his daughter hosts a radio show on WQXR. *Someone's Gotta–*"

"*Someone's Gotta Do It!* Yes! I love that podcast. Harley Solace is an icon," Carlyle says.

"You're familiar with it," I say with a lopsided smile.

"Duh. She's amazing. Her series with that long haul trucker was like a revelation," Carlyle adds.

I look to Resa. She's frowning. "You think we should do an interview on a show that talks to long-haul truckers?"

"No, Resa. That's not the point. She interviews occupations and humanizes them," I say. "And what more do we need right now than humanization? If we give Harley–" I say her name with more familiarity than I'd like, my heart squeezing around the syllables. "Harley Solace, Ms. Solace, if we give her access to one of our actors–"

"We could even have her do it on one of the sound-stages!" Kim says, grinning at Carlyle.

I've got the young people in the room on my side. I know Resa won't have a choice but to agree this is a great idea now. "Yes, a week of interviews here at the studio, giving her access to behind the scenes of one of our shows and clearance to do a comprehensive interview with one of our artists, then–"

"Then we can show our moral high ground through transparency," Resa says as if it's a revelation.

I don't love the sound of that, makes it sound sleazy. But if that's what makes it work for Resa, that's fine with me. "Yes. Exactly."

"You might be onto something, Grant," Resa says with a smirk and then playfully adds, "For once."

I laugh. "Maybe."

From a business perspective, this *is* a great idea. And I can't even say it's selfish. Okay, maybe I want Harley to think about me, just a little. But this might give her show traffic that she's never had before. Traffic that she deserves for her investigative work and bang-up interview skills.

I know, despite every want inside me, that I can't have her. Never again.

That doesn't mean that I can just abandon the thought of her. She's an amazing young woman. If I can offer her opportunities to further her growth and to continue making her way in this world, then that's what I'll do.

There's nothing wrong or dangerous about that, right?

NINE

HARLEY

I'm staring at my Google Calendar, wondering if I'm visibly sweating.

My guest for next week just dropped. I've had them on my calendar for five months now. A deep-sea fishing boat captain whose stories put episodes of *Deadliest Catch* to shame.

I've just received a call that the drama of the high seas has just caught up with them and they've been hospitalized in Juneau for nearly drowning. They're currently vacillating in and out of a coma.

Needless to say, an interview is out of the question.

And that means next week, I'm guestless.

I pull up another window, my LinkedIn page. I use that to connect with people from all different industries. More of the white-collar types. I was really looking forward to digging my hands into the fish guts and drama of the high seas.

But a coma is a coma.

I have a post typed up and ready to go as a call for interview subjects. I haven't had to do this in over a year. My roster filled up so fast once I started the show. Guess I should have counted my blessings. I'll post it on LinkedIn and all my social media, hoping the crazies don't come out.

I proofread it once more, adding a comma and correcting which spelling of "here" I've used. For some reason, I can't bring myself to press post. It feels like taking a step back. Asking for help once you've gotten a certain level of success is wrapped up in more shame than I'd like it to be.

I twiddle my fingers over the keyboard and let out a long sigh. "Just do it..." I whisper.

"What's that?" my workmate and producer, Dre, asks, peeking over his computer at me.

"Nothing," I say with a sheepish smile. "Just talking to myself."

"You do that a lot, don't you?" he says dryly and returns to his computer screen.

I chuckle to myself. Dre is my work husband. We give each other shit constantly. But right now, we're both in the shit, trying to find a new guest. As my producer, he makes sure things go off without a hitch. I know he's beating himself up over losing this guest even though he doesn't control sea storms and comas.

Before I can send out my desperate cry for help through the internet, my desk phone rings. My shoulders slump and I sigh. "What do you think I did this time?" I ask Dre.

"I think the question is what *didn't* you do," Dre replies.

We both eye the phone. *Ring...ring...*

The only calls I ever get to this godforsaken desk phone are from the studio program manager, Gina, who always has a bone to pick with me. You'd think I wasn't the host of the most lucrative daily program at this station. Alas, because of this, her perfectionism is always running me ragged.

I take a deep breath and pick up the phone. "Hello?" I answer in a cheerful voice.

"Is this Harley Solace?"

That voice is *not* Gina's. My eyes snap to Dre. "Um. Yes, this is she."

"*Who is it?*" he mouths.

I glance down at the phone again. If I hadn't been so resigned to my fate of being admonished by Gina for god knows what, I would have noticed that her name wasn't even on the caller ID. It's a protected number.

"This is Resa Blackwell. I'm head of PR for Infinium Entertainment."

My stomach fills with butterflies. This has to be Grant's doing. Why else would his PR team be reaching out to me? "Thanks for calling, Resa. What can I do for you?"

"We're wondering if you would be interested in collaborating with Infinium by bringing one of our artists onto your show."

My heart thuds. I pull up the Google Calendar with the crossed-out guest spot. *Don't sound too eager, Harley.* "I think we could definitely make that happen."

Across my desk, Dre is frowning, demanding more information by mouthing questions. I snap and wave him away. He's distracting me.

"Fantastic. Now, as you know, we have lots of artists on our roster. We'd love to connect you with one of our actors. Maybe a director. That would be at the discretion of your schedule as I assume you're usually booked very far in advance."

Resa is clearly placating to me. Either she really needs this interview to happen or Grant really wants it to happen. I prefer to imagine it's the latter. "Well, you're in luck, I've actually had a guest back out on me for next week and I'm currently looking to fill the spot. Could you arrange for something then?"

She gasps excitedly. "Absolutely! That's better than we could have imagined. I can get back to you with a list of artists with availability for next week in the next fifteen minutes and you can have your pick."

I think about Infinium. All their various shows and reboots. They have half the billboards on the Sunset Strip. It'd be amazing to have someone with so much notoriety appear on the show.

But I think I can do even better than that.

"Actually...do you think it would be possible to get Mr. Neville on the show?"

Dre audibly gasps at my mention of Neville. His name is thrown around as often as Malibu in Hollywood.

Resa's breath stutters. "Beg your pardon?"

"Of course, any of your artists would be welcome..." I say, though I have my mind set on one person and only one. "But to be able to speak to a CEO of a high-powered entertainment company such as Infinium I think would grant listeners such wonderful insight. Would even be a boon to your subscriber base should Mr. Neville be able to pitch the high-quality values of Infinium."

"I can't imagine Mr. Neville has time in his schedule for a *podcast*," she replies in a terse manner, far afield from her friendliness that began the conversation.

I want to spit back, "It's not a podcast," but I hold my tongue. Sure, lots of people listen to the highlights via the podcast Dre puts together. However, it's different. This is a radio show. It's live. And it's uncut and blemished with humanity.

Not a fucking podcast.

I hate to do this. I really hate to after everything. But

now that the idea has crossed my mind, I can't be talked out of it. "Mr. Neville and my dad are good friends," I say through a tense jaw. "They went to college together."

Resa is silent.

"In fact, I know Mr. Neville as well. He's like..." *Oh god.* "Like another member of the family."

Gross, Harley. So gross.

"If you don't feel comfortable asking Mr. Neville to consider this opportunity, I would be happy to ask my father to—"

"No, that won't be necessary," she cuts me off curtly. "What's your father's name? So I can pass it along to Mr. Neville?"

I smile to myself. I know how women like Resa work. They're all nonsense and no fuss but don't want to be caught dead doing something wrong. "Kent Solace. Alpha Phi Alpha." I add their fraternity onto the end to give it a little more of a personal flair.

"Alright. I'll be in touch, Ms. Solace. Thank you."

Before I can respond, she hangs up the call. My stomach drops.

That's not a confirmation, is it? "I'll be in touch." That's a threat. Or lack thereof. Almost like, "Don't call us, we'll call you."

"Well?" Dre asks.

I stare at the receiver. "I think I fucked up."

His brown eyes widen, dark eyebrows raising so high up on his face I'm afraid they'll float away. "You did not let that opportunity slip away."

I swallow.

"Harley!"

"I know, I know, just let me—"

"That was *Infinium Entertainment*. We could have had–"

I knock the receiver against my forehead in shame. "I know."

"Farrah Quinn! Or Wesley Carpenter! Yvette Blanc!"

Three of the biggest names in Hollywood. I could have had any of them. And because of my fucking *hormones* or something, I lost out on not just a confirmed guest for next week, but an amazing show that might make a splash in the national market. "She said she'd call me back..." I say as consolation.

"Yeah, right." Dre snatches the phone out of my hand and slams it down.

But as soon as the phone is back in its cradle, it rings to life again. Dre and I look at each other in absolute shock.

"Answer it!"

I'm already reaching for the phone. "I am!" Not going to worry about seeming eager anymore. I want this. More than anything. "H-hello?"

"Mr. Neville has agreed to an interview."

My jaw drops. Honestly, I'm shocked he has agreed. For one, he's a busy man. For another, I thought he'd want to keep me as far from him as possible. Maybe he hasn't had to deal with the fallout like I have. Maybe he's been able to move past the feelings of desire and yearning for me.

I, on the other hand, have been trapped by wanting Grant. At every moment of every day.

Keep it professional. It's work, not play. I clear my throat. "That's...fantastic to hear."

Dre leaps up from his seat and covers his mouth to celebrate quietly.

"There is just one condition. Mr. Neville's schedule is very busy, I'm sure you can understand that."

"Of course, of course."

"We can offer you one extended interview."

I nod, though she can't see me. "That'll work just fine. We can release it in pieces throughout the week." While it's not my preferred way to do things, I've done it when I have a guest I just can't lose. Four hours straight with a guest can be grueling, but if that's what gets Grant into my studio, that works perfectly for my purposes.

Perfectly, in a world where I'm looking to sabotage myself at every turn.

"Great. Look out for an email from me. We will be in touch regarding logistics."

"Yes. Thank you so much."

"You're welcome so much."

She hangs up again. *Okay, rude.*

There's no time to languish in her shortness before Dre pulls me up from my chair and starts jumping up and down with me. "You did it! You got it!"

We embrace, relief flowing through our bodies. No more scrambling on social media to find a guest. We're set for next week.

Though there are plenty of anxieties bubbling up in the background, I cannot deny my excitement over seeing Grant again.

Just me and him. In the booth. Talking.

I'll have to be on my best behavior.

And that's a challenge I can't wait to take on.

TEN

GRANT

I can't believe I'm doing this. I can't believe I'm sitting here across from Harley Solace in a recording booth at WQXR, preparing to be interviewed by her.

The big headphones on her ears make her look adorably little. Yet, not for a second does she look immature. From the moment I walk into the station, Harley is in her element, directing people where to go and what to do.

Don't get me wrong, it's awkward. Incredibly so. When I walked in, neither of us knew how to greet each other. In fact, I could barely speak, just as when she greeted me at the Fourth of July party. She takes my breath away with her mere presence. Her natural beauty, not tainted with makeup, is enough to bowl me over and send me into silence.

Thank god she picked up where I failed and greeted me with a simple, "Hi, how are you?" We barely exchanged two sentences before her overexcited producer interrupted us to make an introduction. Harley seemed nonplussed.

Perhaps I've been making a bigger deal out of all of this

than it actually is. If this attraction is unrequited, that would be for the best, even if it breaks my heart the tiniest bit.

From the way she's carrying herself, she seems unfazed that I'm here. Checking audio levels and doing a few vocal warm-ups, I may as well not be in the room.

"Alright, I think we're ready," Harley says into the mic. It's like she's right next to me rather than across the table with how her voice cuts through. "Need anything?" she asks, her brown eyes finding mine amidst the jungle of equipment.

I gulp. Need lots of things from her. And need isn't too strong a word. My desire for her is so strong. I know we agreed it would never happen again, but I can't help but wonder if it did, what would happen? "I think I'm good."

"More water?" Harley nods toward my glass. "We'll take a couple of breaks, but the first hour is usually the most difficult. Getting used to..." She gestures toward the room. "Everything."

I chuckle and shake my head. "I'm alright on water. Thank you."

Part of what made meeting her at the party so staggering was realizing what a beautiful woman she had turned into. Now, I get to see her in all that grown glory. Taking on the world, one interview at a time.

You might wonder why I accepted this interview when I know the best thing for me to do would be to stay away from her.

Admittedly, when Resa asked, I didn't hesitate to agree. I hadn't brought up the idea of an interview thinking that Harley would want to interview *me*. It was a way of keeping her close and at arm's length at the same time.

So, I was surprised to find out she was interested in talking to me. I hardly ever give interviews outside the purview of my company. I know this one will be a bit more in-depth than I'm used to giving.

I can't imagine a better person for the job than Harley.

"This might not be live, but we're doing each hour in one take. That alright with you? No restarting answers or pretending like you didn't say something," Harley explains with a smirk.

Or pretending like I didn't do something? "Don't worry, I did my research. I'm prepared."

Her eyebrows jump briefly before she looks through the window separating the booth and the board. "Alright, count us in, Dre."

"Grant Neville interview part one. Harley go in three...two..."

No "one". Dre simply points to Harley. And suddenly, she alights as if someone has flipped her switch. "Hi, I'm Harley Solace. Past Harley, not the live version. And this is *Someone's Gotta Do It*, where I come to you five days a week to pull back the curtain on careers across sector boundaries to show you just how hard America is working."

I have no doubt she's said this hundreds of times, but it doesn't come off as overly rehearsed. It's as if she's talking to an old friend on the phone.

"This week's guest is very special, so special we could only take up his time for one day as opposed to our usual five. I'll be talking with the CEO and founder of Infinium Entertainment, Grant Neville."

She pauses and I'm wondering if I'm supposed to be introducing myself. She quickly starts to speak again. "Yes, I had to leave air for the gasps and applause."

I laugh and hope it's not too loud on the recording.

"None of this could have been made possible without our sponsors at Rebus Mattress: Mattresses For Life. And, admittedly, nepotism," Harley adds with a waggle of her eyebrows. "Grant, why don't you tell the audience how we know each other?"

I can appreciate that she wants to be transparent with her listeners. However, to ask *me* to characterize our relationship makes my pulse race. "I've known your father since college."

"Alpha Phi Alpha," she says in a singsong voice.

"Yes, that was our fraternity at USC."

"You've known my dad since before I was born," Harley says.

My jaw drops. Was that meant to be pointed? I can't tell. She's looking at me directly. But it doesn't seem like a challenge. Just a fact.

Just like it's a fact that we never should have fucked.

Just like it's a fact that I'd like to fuck her again.

Get your head out of the clouds. Bring it back down to earth. "Um, yes. I actually remember when you were born."

Harley laughs, her eyes rolling to the side. Is she blushing? "Well, that's a story for another time. We're not here to talk about me. We're here to talk about you."

"I can't imagine I'd be a very good interviewer. Not like you are."

"Flattery, Mr. Neville, will get you everywhere."

Now this feels like banter. A back and forth. A flirtation.

I've got to stay calm. This is on recording. And there's no backtracking. That's important. Everything I say is going to be included just the way I say it.

"How fast can I jump in?" Harley asks.

Our eyes meet. Now that *is* a challenge. She wants to know if she can go from zero to sixty, jump into the questions she wants to know, the juicy details about how I run my successful media empire. Not unlike how the two of us went from zero to sixty with our attraction. We're good at that.

Who am I to stop her?

"This is your show, Harley. You're in charge."

A grin spreads across her lips. "Excellent."

Hour one was a focus on the scope of Infinium as it stands as a company today. It was in-depth and well-researched.

Hour two is about my role as founder and CEO. Harley isn't afraid to challenge me when she hears a philosophy she doesn't agree with. And I'm not afraid to give it right back. It's all good fun. She had a smile on her face nearly the entire time.

As did I.

Hour three is about the future of the company. Where I want to go. Where *she* thinks it should go. That's a fun conversation. I'm transported back in time to the party, when things were simpler, but budding and bubbling under the surface. Where the viciousness of my attraction really began. She's sassy and stubborn in her opinions. I can tell she likes to be challenged just as much as she challenges.

I could love a woman like that.

Not Harley, obviously. But a woman who is passionate and opinionated, who can think about the big picture as well as care about the small.

I don't find a lot of that in LA.

And yet, as the interview goes on, I can't help but imagine a life with Harley. Our eyes are locked practically the whole time. She's making me feel like I'm the only man in the world. It's the eternal, subtle smile on her lips and the cock of her head. She's really listening to me, drawing more out of me with just the tiny look in her eye.

She probably makes every interviewee feel like that. But has she fucked every one of her interviewees? Doubtful, unless that's some weird underbelly of this show I don't quite know yet.

Beyond what's happening in the booth, I can tell it's going well from the way her producer is leaning on his elbows watching us. He's captivated.

And so am I. With her voice coming through my headphones, I feel like we're lying together as I imagined we could have after our roll in the hay. We could have spread out on the blankets lining the treehouse floor and enjoyed the closeness a bit longer.

Instead, we were rudely interrupted.

Maybe that's why she's feeling a little distant. Perhaps the abrupt exit and the impossibility of aftercare made her feel used up and unappreciated. God, I hope that's not it.

Now, it's hour four. Hour four is "grab bag". That's usually the Thursday episode from the series I've listened to. The Friday episode is dedicated to Harley's take aways as well as conversations with listeners. I'm already dreading what they might say about me.

There's a reason I don't do many interviews. People generally don't like me. I'm wealthy, I'm powerful, and I'm in charge of the media that people watch. There's something in there to anger every demographic.

Alas, I agreed.

So far, I'm glad I did.

"Alright, Grant," Harley says, having been counted into the fourth hour. "This is my bag." She pulls up an orange velvet bag. "My literal grab bag. It has many questions, ranging from–"

"'What's your perfect day?' to 'What inspires you?'" I say, quoting the intro she gives every time. "I know. I'm a fan."

Harley puts the bag down on the table, her mouth slightly ajar. "I thought you just listened to a couple for research."

"Well, yes, I did. But I also have...become a bit of a fan," I say with a nervous chuckle. She doesn't need to know I've listened to half of this year's episodes since I saw her at the beginning of July.

She smiles and shakes her head in disbelief. "Wow. Okay. Can't say I get very many fans on here." She looks at Dre. I can tell she's embarrassed. But the grateful kind of embarrassed.

I'm more than proud to be the one to make her blush. Even if it's not in the way I've been dreaming of night after night.

Harley clears her throat and adjusts her headphones. "Alright, then you know how this goes."

"I do. May I?" I ask, holding my hand out across the table.

Harley eyes it momentarily. I almost think she's going to grab it. That would be more than I could bear. I'm hard just thinking about her touch. Thank god it's under the table. But no, just as she should, she hands the grab bag over.

"I'll reach into the bag, pull out a sheet of paper, and that will be our topic until we run out of things to talk about," I say with a flourish. The joke of this is that a single question seems to get every guest all the way through the grab-bag hour. Harley is just that talented of an interviewer. Can see angles and edges no one else can see.

"You really are a fan, huh?"

I reach my hand into the bag and smile, "You didn't believe me."

She crosses her arms over her chest and leans back in her chair. "Don't forget to shake the bag around in the mic for effect."

"Oh, yes, how could I?" I speak. I hold the bag up to the mic and shuffle it around, so it picks up the sound of papers shuffling around inside.

Harley giggles. Oh, how I love to make her laugh. It warms the coil in my belly every time.

I pinch a piece of paper in my hands and withdraw it. "Drum roll, please."

Harley hits the table with her hands as I unfold the paper.

The second I see the word "love" on the paper, the blood drains out of my face.

"You good?"

I realize I've been staring at the paper for a couple of seconds and that's a couple of seconds too long for radio. "Um..."

"Don't keep us on the edge of our seats," Harley encourages. "Read it."

I take a deep breath. "The question is..." My eyes land in hers almost by accident. Almost. "Do you believe in love?"

All at once, she understands my silence. Harley's eyes widen, her mouth sealed shut.

What happened between us...that wasn't love. But it wasn't an absence of love altogether.

"Well...uh..." Harley forces a laugh. "Can't say we've ever had that one." She repositions herself in her chair. "Been dreading it, honestly. Dre made me put it in."

Dre grins and gives a thumbs up from the board.

"We can pick another one," I say, hurriedly returning the paper to the grab bag.

"No, we can't. Not how the bag works." Harley sighs and leans forward, clasping her hands on the table as if we're about to start a business transaction rather than a conversation. "Well, Grant." Her warm brown eyes are giving me a fever just by looking at me. "Do you believe in love?"

I half-laugh and rub my hand over my chin in thought. I cleaned up my beard this morning knowing I was going to see Harley. Wanted to make a good impression. "What kind of love are we talking about?"

"Romantic," she answers plainly. Whether or not she meant it to be implicit in the question doesn't matter. That's what she wants to know about.

"Well, at the risk of sounding like a misanthrope," I say and then give a small shrug, "I think any kind of romantic love is a farce."

Harley is quiet and then smiles brightly. "Well, that's something we can agree on."

I'm relieved. Or am I?

"Tell me more about that, Grant."

"What do you want to know?"

Harley gesticulates, a pen in her hand. "You know, just tell me more. Why do you think that?"

"I could ask you the same."

"But I'm the interviewer!" she says with a grin.

I try to laugh but it just comes out limp like a balloon losing air. "Let me just say that I don't think that means we shouldn't try and connect with people. You know, dating and—"

"Sex."

She's knocked the wind right out of me with just one word. Now I know she's thinking about it at the same moment I am, the amazing way our bodies came together. She's putting a spotlight on it. "Are you allowed to say sex on public radio?"

"This is talk radio. The lines are blurred."

Yes, they are blurred indeed. The line between what's inappropriate and appropriate. The line between friend and lover. "I'm not saying we should all be celibate and shouldn't try to find connection. I've just seen things that people have put under the guise of love that I just don't think are love at all."

Harley nods. "Like–"

"Violence. And anger. People claim that there's this thing called love that gives them license to act without rationality and without thinking about what their actions might do to harm other people and..." All of a sudden, I hear myself. Fuck. I've harmed in the name of love. Not *love* love. But I'm staring at the woman I didn't resist even though if the truth came to light, we would be hurting someone close to both of us.

Harley raises an eyebrow. "Go on."

It feels like she's taunting me, daring me to say something that I might regret. I'm cornered, a skittering animal held captive by a vixen. The past three hours I wanted nothing more than to be under her spell forever.

Now I want to jump out of my skin.

"Wait a second," I say. "You don't believe in love either."

"This isn't about me, it's–"

"Why?"

Harley moves back in her chair as if I've just slapped her in the face. "*Why?*"

I know that she's seen love fall apart. What happened between her parents would fuck anyone up for the rest of their life. I'm not trying to get her to speak to that. What I want to know is much more nuanced. "You're so young, Harley."

She furrows her brow. "So?"

"So...how much can you really have seen to make you think love isn't real?"

"I...uh, wow," Harley looks away, scratching her cheek.

"I've had a lifetime to reflect on what's broken about this thing called 'love'. You've had twenty-six years." Gosh, she's so young. She's so fucking young and I've spent all this time fantasizing about her. I'd be robbing her of something if I continued to pursue her.

Harley shakes her head, eyes fluttering shut. "You don't know anything about me."

"That's not true."

"It is. You don't know anything about me at all. And for you to sit there and act like somehow your experiences regarding love and farce are more important than mine—"

"Hold on, I didn't say more important."

"*Valuable!*" she shouts back.

I see Dre visibly wince in the booth. She's blown both our eardrums out.

"You think time makes your life experience more valuable. Is that right?" Harley looks at me, her face having fallen. I've never seen her like this. Corners of her lips falling, rims of her eyes red.

I've hit a nerve. Exposed a whole set of them. "Forgive me. I...that's not what I meant by that." There's no use excusing myself. I've hurt her. The last thing I'd ever want to do.

Consequently, I've hurt myself as well. I wish I could absorb the pain I've just caused her, take it all back.

It's too late.

"Pick a new question," Harley says in a fraying voice.

I guess I'll be the first second question in the grab bag history.

And that's not an accomplishment I'm proud of.

ELEVEN
HARLEY

Saying that the episode goes over well would be an understatement. My interview with Grant Neville is the most talked about episode in the history of my show *period*. I'm getting coverage on national morning shows and even getting some international interest as well.

I have to wonder at what cost, though.

Because seeing Grant again, being in his vicinity, and feeling his aura...stirred all the feelings I'd been trying to keep down.

Don't get me wrong, our conversation about love was all I needed to know that Grant and me together would be an absolute trainwreck. As if I didn't know that before. Though our opinions on love match to a t, it's clear he doesn't respect my experience based on my age. I won't put up with that.

No way, no how.

However, Grant has now become my calling card. Everyone wants to know how I snagged the interview. I'm honest with them. I know a guy and that guy happens to be my dad. Then they want to know what he was like. And I have to describe to people what Grant is like, veiling any feelings of desire I've had for him. It's enough to drive a person mad.

I've also gotten some hate online for featuring Grant on the show.

Didn't realize we were trying to humanize billionaires now, is one comment that sticks out in my mind like a sore thumb.

The goal of my show is to humanize everybody. Because...that's what we all are. Humans.

I try to ignore the haters.

This effort is made easier when Gina is so fucking impressed with me. She won't shut up about my star turn of an interview with Grant Neville.

I have to say, it's nice to have the program manager wanting to talk to me in a positive way for once.

"Listen, the Auras are tomorrow night and they reached out because they had an award presenter drop," Gina says while focused on stirring up her overnight oats. "They want you to do it."

I blink, unsure if I'm trapped in a dream. "Uh, what?"

"You heard me, Harley, don't act like you didn't hear me," Gina replies.

I watch her chew on a spoonful of cold oats while I consider what she's just said. The Auras are only a few years old but they're the foremost awards in audio broadcasting, acknowledging all modern mediums including podcasts, audiobooks, radio shows...the list goes on. They're not televised like the Grammys or Oscars, but they're at that level. To win an Aura is a crowning achievement.

"Who knows, maybe this season you can submit your episode with Grant Neville for consideration," Gina goes on, mouth full of oats. She swallows loudly. "So, will you do it?"

"Y-yes! Yes. Absolutely."

"Great," she grins. There's a chia seed stuck between her front two teeth. "I'll forward you all the information."

As I leave her office, my heart races with excitement and nerves. This is a big deal. Even if I'm not nominated myself, I'm *presenting*.

Then it hits me. I have to find something to wear. And *fast*.

AFTER WORK, I hurry out to meet with Kira. Though she's the quiet one and the most practical with her style, she has the best eye for color. Plus, she keeps it real. If something looks nice, she always makes sure it's actually comfortable. I've been saved many times by Kira's logic.

We end up settling on a slinky green dress with a mock turtleneck that makes me look like a snake about to shed its skin. It's thin enough that I won't burn up under the studio lights and fitted enough that it shows off all of my assets.

Who knows? Maybe I'll meet someone who will take my mind and my body off Grant Neville.

However, tonight, just as many nights before, I dream of him.

In the weeks following our first encounter, my mind kept replaying our time in the treehouse to varying degrees of weirdness. Sometimes the treehouse was floating in midair, other times our bodies would start to fade into each other. Every time, however, we were having sex. And the dreams were always euphoric.

This one is different.

I'm in control. I can tell I'm in a dream. I don't have to guess, don't have to worry.

We're in the studio. *My* studio. Sitting across from each other.

"Do you believe in love?" Grant asks me, except because it's a dream, his words come out like he's talking through water, muffled and warbling.

I go to say no, but I can't speak. "No," I try to say, but all that comes out is hoarse air. "*No,*" I try to say again but this time I actually say, "*Yes.*"

That's not true. I don't believe in love.

Do I?

Suddenly, all the equipment is gone. The table is bare. It's just Grant and me looking at each other, our hands pressed to the tabletop, waiting for someone to make the first move.

He reaches under the table and flips it as if it takes no strength at all. As the table falls, it turns into a bed. And in the blink of an eye, I'm sitting on the edge of it.

I look up and Grant is standing before me, but my vision is blurred like I've gone cross-eyed.

"Grant?"

He steps closer and closer. As he comes more into focus, I notice that he's naked. From top to bottom. Beautiful, tan and toned body with swirls of hair across his chest. His hands are balled into fists. And before my eyes can reach his package, he kneels at the edge of the bed and touches my thighs.

I'm naked. I don't remember getting naked, but I am.

And I'm not afraid.

His hands knead my thighs as his eyes travel up my body. A look of desperation and pain in his blue eyes. His brow is furrowed. He's...aching.

I reach out and touch my hands to his forehead, softening out the wrinkles. Grant closes his eyes and his mouth falls open in relief. Just my touch has relieved some of this pain. This mental turmoil.

I've been feeling it too. The pressure of doing something so wrong. Of wanting to do it again.

"We shouldn't," he whispers.

"I know," I say, but while my mind knows we can't, my body will not listen. His skin is as smooth as butter.

"Not again."

We've already done it once. That can be considered a mistake. Twice would be a coincidence. Three times a pattern.

But does any of that count in dreams?

No. This is where I get to live out my fantasy instead of continuing to ruin my reality.

"But I have to," I whisper and lean down to kiss him.

Grant accepts my lips without any hesitation. He was resisting for show, not because he really wanted to.

Plus, this is my dream. He'll do what I want him to do.

I wrap my hands around his head, raking my fingers through his dark curls. So soft. Everything about him is so soft. Even though in life he is hard. The jaw, the chest, the brittle texture of the gray hairs at his temples.

Here, he is the softest thing I have ever touched.

Though this is my dream and I'm in control, my brain can still surprise me. Grant pulls on my thighs and forces me onto my back. "I need to taste you."

"Oh god..." I moan, wriggling my hips up toward his needful mouth.

Grant trails kisses up the inside of my thigh. I can feel his hot breath on my center, wet with want. "I smell you wherever I go."

I bend my head.

"Wherever you go, I'll find you."

He's like an animal, able to track me down from miles away. It terrifies me in the best way. Because if Grant can find me wherever I am, that means that we are intrinsically connected. Not just by familiarity. But by something *much, much greater*.

Grant presses his mouth against my pussy and begins to devour me, lips and tongue roving against my swollen center.

I moan but no sound comes out, hoarse once again. I try to scream in pleasure, but still, nothing comes out.

My mind is determined to remind me that this is a dream. It's not reality. It will never feel as freeing as the real thing.

Because for the real thing to happen again, that means I've shed all fear, all sense of decorum, all respect and loyalty to my father.

For the real thing to happen, I will have had to give into the part of myself I've been hiding.

I will have to be satisfied with dreams for now.

Grant laps up my juices, runs his tongue against my clit, humming harder and harder and harder until –

My orgasm wakes me up. I'm sweating so much that I think my air conditioner might have kicked off in the middle of the night. However, I can hear it droning in the background. I kick off the sheets and fall back asleep, trying to ignore a prayer in the back of my mind for Grant to return to my dreams.

"I'M NERVOUS."

"Don't be. You look amazing."

Dre and I have just sat down at our table at the Auras. I brought him as my date. It was the only thing that made sense. After all, I don't know if I would have gotten to this level of success without him as my trusty, unfettered producer.

He's right. I do look amazing. The dress fits like a glove, I had my makeup and hair professionally done, and photographers have been eating me up all night.

But here, with all the tables full of talent, it's hard to not feel like I'm the smallest fish in this big pond.

The Auras bring people from all corners of the entertainment industry together. Actors, writers, musicians, producers. Sky is the limit. To my right is a group of writers from the amazing audio drama *Tivoly and Friends*, to my left is OpalWest, an indie band whose music I've come to adore, and right in front of me is—

Holy shit.

"Harley? You okay? You look like you've seen a ghost."

Not a ghost. Much worse. Because straight ahead of us at the table front and center stands Grant Neville. Looking...perfect. Just like always. He's wearing a tailored suit I bet is more expensive than a month of my apartment's rent. He isn't wearing a tie, nothing stodgy. He's left his tight white button-down undone just enough to expose some of his chest hair. Holy shit, I'd love to just rip it off of him and lick every inch of his body.

I might be tempted to go say hi if not for one glaring issue: he's pulling out a chair for a woman with her hair swept back in a slick bun, not a singular hair out of place.

My heart drops so low I think it might have just fallen out of my body.

Grant is here. And he's brought a date.

"No reason," I say quickly, looking down at the place setting in front of us. "These are nice plates," I remark. *Seriously, Harley? You're not selling this.*

"Oh, shit, there's Grant!" Dre says.

"What, are you two on a first-name basis?" I ask with a bit too much spit and vinegar.

Dre ignores my comment and starts to get up. "I'm going to go say hi."

I grab his sportscoat and yank him back into his seat. "Don't!"

"Jesus! What the fuck, Harley!"

"Sorry, I..." I glance back at Grant and his date. I can tell she's beautiful just from the back. Older than me probably. More mature. Just like he might want. For...well, not forever, since he doesn't believe in love. But for now. "He's with someone. We shouldn't interrupt." God, why am I jealous? We aren't together. Could never be. We both can do whatever and whomever we want.

I can't ignore that I want *him*, though. Those gorgeous curls, shiny with product and volume, call for me to touch them.

"Everyone is talking to everyone, Harley, you're being weird." Dre starts to get up again, but I grab his arm.

"Dre, please, I'm so nervous and I just need you to... to..." I trail off as Grant's date turns around. I nearly laugh when I realize who it is. "Oh, that's Victoria Neville."

Dre alerts again like he's a bloodhound on the search. "The supermodel?"

"Yes, the supermodel. His sister!" I say through a laugh, clutching my heart. I shouldn't be so relieved, but I am.

Just because *I* can't have him doesn't mean I want anyone else to.

"I'll introduce you," I say to Dre. "Later. For now. Just... calm me down."

Dre smiles and rolls his eyes. "Fine."

Little does he know that he'll be calming me down from much more than presenting an award. He's going to be talking me down from the ledge that wants to throw myself right at Grant Neville and fuck his brains out.

"Okay, listen to me, Flick–" I grab onto the actor's shoulders and look into his hazel eyes. "I need you to read from the cue cards exactly as they're written."

Flick nods. "I got it, boss."

"No, no. You don't got it," I reply. I've corralled Flick into the corner of the talent holding room backstage. This is Flick's first event since his scandal broke. A low-level awards show. It may not be televised, but the media is still here. And I know all eyes are going to be on Flick. "You can't deviate from the script. No editorializing, no embellishing, no–"

"Relax, Neville," Flick says in his California surfer way, running a hand through his blonde curly hair that for some reason looks wet and crusty at the same time. "This isn't a big deal, I promise."

I force a smile. I promised Resa I would do my due diligence and not let him do anything stupid. Unfortunately, with Flick, it's hard to ever anticipate what this guy is going to do. "It's a very big deal, Flick. This is your first public appearance since...you know, everything. And I'm counting on you not to make Infinium look–"

"Stupid. I know." Flick grins. "I promise, Grant, I won't–"

Suddenly, we're interrupted by the announcer: "Presenting the award for best-unscripted radio program, up-and-coming radio personality and host, Harley Solace."

My focus on Flick shatters. Harley Solace? That's a one-of-a-kind name. There aren't any others in LA, let alone any who are up-and-coming radio hosts.

Against my better judgment, I abandon Flick in the green room and go backstage. It's entirely quiet back here. The only thing I can hear is Harley.

"It's my honor to present the award for best-unscripted radio program. The nominees are..."

As she lists the nominees, I peer through the wings and onto the stage. Holy shit. She looks dynamite. I don't know how I didn't notice she was here already given that she looks like a fucking Grecian goddess. Her short blonde hair has been styled in tight curls and her skin glows golden. And that dress...goddamn, my imagination doesn't do her body justice.

"Neville?" I hear Flick whisper at my shoulder.

"Huh–what?" I don't even pay him a look. I'm captivated by Harley.

"We good?"

"Yeah, just...read the cards," I say without another thought. Flick is going to do what Flick is going to do. Nothing I can say or do will stop that. At least that's the justification I'm going to use so I can just stare at Harley Solace.

Flick watches Harley beside me. "Damn, she's a babe. You know her?"

I glare at him. I want to say, "Don't even think about it," but that might be showing my hand. "Daughter of a friend."

"You think you could introduce me?"

"Aren't you going through a divorce?" I shoot back bitterly.

Flick glowers. "You don't have to rub it in."

Now I'm fully done with Flick. The only thing I care about is the glowing goddess on stage, looking as glimmery as an award herself.

I've been thinking about Harley nonstop since the interview. We ended on such a strange note after our conversation about love. She barely even looked at me when I said goodbye, opting instead to start listening to playback in the booth with her producer. All I got was a wave and a pitiful smile.

I chalked her distance up to my indiscretion. Mentioning her age was...wrong of me. Regardless of what I think or my questions, I shouldn't have devalued all her experiences just because she might have been young when they happened. I don't know her whole life. Her *whole* story.

I know that everything that happened with her mother must have caused her a lot of pain. But from the look in her eyes, the pain, I think there is more to the story.

I have found myself wishing for her trust. For her honesty. It's all so wrong, feels more wrong every passing day that I still desire her and wish for her to be in my life.

Now, here she is. A mere coincidence.

Or a fated encounter.

"And the award goes to..." she opens up a golden envelope, "*Live with Daisy*."

The applause resounds as Daisy Sinclair, host of the show, climbs the stage for her acceptance speech. Harley

hands her the award and they exchange a hug and a kiss on the cheek before Harley starts to walk offstage.

Her eyes immediately land on me. I notice the hesitation in her feet. But she has no choice but to walk right to me unless she wants to make a scene at this awards show.

With each step she takes toward me, I stand a little taller. What should I say? What should I do? I don't want to make her uncomfortable, but I can't just let her walk by without–

Any plan I have is immediately scrapped when Harley hits the wings and walks right past me without so much as a smile.

What the fuck?

I turn to Flick and give him a pat on the arm. "You'll do great. Just stick to the cards."

"You got it, Neville."

I don't care if this man starts shouting a string of expletives on stage at this point. I need to talk to Harley.

I turn around and see that she's talking with one of the stage managers with a friendly smile. I can tell she's trying to walk away but the SM is holding her captive, talking her ear off. Perfect. She's a captive audience.

"I just love your show. I try to listen to it live, but sometimes–"

"Just listening to it at all means a lot," Harley says, pulling at her skirt, ready to dart away.

"I loved the one with the plumber. I had no idea how talented they have to be!"

Harley laughs nervously. Her eyes flick to me. She's been spotted and can't run.

"Excuse me, may I interrupt?" I ask.

The stage manager looks at me with big eyes. "Of

course, Mr. Neville." Then, she looks at Harley, "I also loved your episode with Mr. Neville."

"You're very kind," Harley says. There's an edge of discomfort in her voice. I know it's my fault. "It's good to see you, Mr. Neville."

Mr. Neville. That makes me sound like a middle school biology teacher. Not her friend. Her former lover. "Yes, always a pleasure to run into you." I eye the stage manager; she gets the hint and skitters off to deal with Flick before he goes on to present his award. "You mind if we talk for a minute? Somewhere private."

Harley's body goes rigid. For a moment, I think she's going to refuse, but then she nods. "Alright."

"Perfect." I nod in the direction of the green room. "This way."

I touch the small of Harley's back to guide her in that direction. She glances up at me in surprise. "You lead," she says, stepping out of my touch.

Fine. That's fair. I overstepped too quickly. I clear my throat and push my hands into my pockets. "Very well."

I lead Harley into the green room which is empty now. I don't want to risk us being interrupted, though, so I take it a step further and open the door to the private dressing room along the back wall. "After you."

Harley steps through, the lights automatically turning on. I close the door behind us and resist locking it. I don't want to give her the wrong impression.

I'm not going to lie to myself: if the opportunity presented itself, I'd have her again here and now. But I'm not going to force it. In fact, I'm going to actively resist it as long as I can.

Until my body can't take it anymore.

"What would you like to talk about, Grant?" Harley

asks. She's leaning up against the makeup table, the vanity lights casting her in a warm, intoxicating light.

"I..." I sigh heavily. *Don't beat around the bush. You've been inside her, for god's sake. No use holding anything back now.* "I feel like I owe you an apology for our conversation on your show."

Harley frowns.

"I shouldn't have mentioned your age. It was...disrespectful." I'm trying to maintain eye contact with her but it's too hard when I know what her eyes do to me. "I don't know what your experiences have been. Other than...well–"

"Grant, it's okay," she says. "You hit a nerve. That's all. I shouldn't have been so dramatic. I don't know what got into me, honestly." Harley looks down at the tips of her gold pumps. "Maybe because we...there's history there, I think I was just feeling raw."

History. Lots of it. Eighteen years of her life and then one night to turn it all upside down.

"I should have known that inviting you to the studio would make me feel..." Harley stops and then shakes her head. "Anyway, it's water under the bridge."

"I hope that you weren't hurt by what happened on the Fourth of July."

Her eyes widen. "Hurt? Oh no. No, that's not what I meant, not at all."

"Okay, good. I wouldn't want you to have walked away from that feeling like I'd taken advantage of you or made you feel uncomfortable, or..." I'm talking too much. "Yeah."

Harley half-laughs. "No, it was the exact opposite. It was...I haven't been able to stop thinking about it."

Harley's brave. Braver than me. She just came right out and said what I've been thinking for over a month now. "Me too," I say, voice slight and strained.

In most circumstances, the revelation of mutual attraction would be cause for celebration. For us, it's painful. I can see as much as Harley furrows her brow and groans. "Fuck."

"Yeah. Fuck," I say, chuckling.

"You weren't supposed to say that."

"What was I supposed to say?"

"I don't know!" she says, crossing her arms over her chest. "We were just supposed to ignore it and move on. Because it never should have happened."

I nod. "You're right. Never should have happened."

"Because—"

"Yep."

Our eyes meet. "My dad."

I didn't need her to say it to know that's what she was referring to. But maybe bringing him into the conversation makes this more real. Maybe then we can't get away with pretending we don't know better. "I never meant to make it hard on you, by—"

"I know. Me either. For you."

Silence. I can't ignore her beauty. I'm a monster.

"I feel so guilty."

"Me too."

Harley lets out a long, frustrated sigh. "It's even worse because I know I'd do it again if I could."

Me too, I think. If I say it out loud, I'm afraid we will just come together like angry magnets, our bodies finding homes in each other that we've both been searching for this past month.

"I guess it's probably worse for you."

"I'm not going to play 'who has it worse', but I do feel like I should know better," I say. I shove my hands in my

pockets to keep them occupied instead of thinking about how her breasts might fill my palms. "I'm older after all."

"*Way* older."

"Hey!" I retort playfully.

Harley laughs. It's the first moment she's seemed relaxed this whole time, throwing her head back, mouth open with laughter. "You know what I mean."

I nod. "I do." Despite knowing what's good for me, I take a step forward. "If your dad wasn't involved, would you...could we..."

"No," she answers firmly.

That cuts deeper than I'd have imagined.

Harley shuts her eyes tight. "Sorry, that came out harsher than I meant it."

"It's alright. It's fair."

"I just mean..." She takes a deep breath. "I know what it's like to be so different in age from someone and it just doesn't work."

I want to ask for more information. However, it's clear divulging even that much is a feat for her.

"Besides. My dad is involved. You're his best friend."

I gulp. I *am* his best friend. That's a big responsibility. Especially when my best friend has been betrayed by someone so close to him before. It's my responsibility to be loyal to him.

Sleeping with his daughter, lusting after her, putting her on a pedestal, is *not* the cornerstone of loyalty.

"I am. And you're his daughter," I say.

Harley manages to lock eyes with me. Strong. Unflinching. "Yeah, I am."

This feels like the natural conclusion to our conversation. "Well–"

Apparently, I'm wrong. Or I'm right in that it *is* the end

of our conversation. However, something else begins when Harley launches herself across the room toward me, flings her arms around my neck, and kisses me harshly.

I gasp into her lips, stumbling back against the door from her force. "Holy...shit..." I say breathlessly between kisses. "Harley..."

"Don't you want to?"

I have to stifle a loud laugh. "Trust me, I want to." My nose knocks up against hers. "Will we regret it, though?"

Harley pauses and then shakes her head. "I won't." She grinds her hips against mine and I feel my member stir to life. "Will you?"

"No," I reply without hesitation.

Harley locks the door and then raises her lusty brown eyes to mine. "Touch me, Grant."

I slide my hands down her back, around the curve of her ass. Her dress is so thin it's almost like I'm touching her bare body.

Harley runs her hands up my chest. "We should be quick," she whispers.

"I'll take as long as I like," I say gruffly. I've been thinking about this for too long to restrain myself.

Harley giggles, "Whatever you say."

She's taken control at first and now it's my turn. I push her by her hips up against the vanity table and yank her legs forward so our pelvises stay connected, then ravenously kiss her. Harley runs her hands through my hair. Her fingernails against my scalp give me goosebumps.

"It's not fair," I murmur, pushing her skirt up to reveal her smooth, luscious legs.

"What's not fair?" she giggles.

"How fucking gorgeous you look tonight. How beautiful you are," I say and pinch her chin between my fingers.

Honestly, her beauty leaves me speechless. Her blushing lips, pert nose, thick eyelashes. "Seriously, Harley, how am I supposed to resist you?"

She leans her head back against the mirror with a lazy smile, locking her legs around my hips. "You're not."

"God, I didn't know you were such a bad girl, Harley," I mutter as I hook my finger through her thong. It's just a useless piece of fabric at this point, completely soaked through by her essence. "I want to taste you."

"No time. Just fuck me," she drawls desperately.

I wish I could take my time. I'd eat her out so good. She'd be so weak she wouldn't even be able to say my name. And I just know that she'll taste amazing. But she's right. We're locked in a dressing room backstage at an event full of lots of people we want to make good impressions on. The last thing we want to do is get caught and have any of the media speculating about anything.

Harley reaches out and undoes the closure on my pants, tilting her head back to look into my eyes as she does so. When she wraps her hand around my cock, I sigh with pleasure. Her palm is so warm and her grip is just tight enough. Harley bites on her lower lip. "Been thinking about you filling me every day."

Filling. What a fucking fantastic word. "I've been thinking about it too," I say.

Harley pushes her hips up to meet mine, adjusts my cock to find her entrance, and pushes her hips forward. Takes everything in me not to just let my knees buckle. I have to be strong. I'm in charge after all.

"Holy shit, you feel so good," I grunt, sliding in and out of her slowly. Stretching her.

Harley reaches over her head and grabs onto the ridge

of the mirror against the wall. "Fuck me, Grant. Fuck me, *please.*"

"You're already begging."

She shakes her head from side to side, clearly already in the midst of euphoria. "I need you. I need you to fill me."

There's that word again. *Fill.* I pulse my hips faster, cock filling her up over and over. Might she mean a different type of fill? The dangerous kind? The kind where I might spill inside her and cause an accident?

A beautiful accident, but still. One that would be hard to take back.

Harley interrupts my train of thought by grabbing onto my shoulders and pulling herself closer to me so our foreheads touch. "I need you, Grant. I need you," she says through clenched teeth.

With each thrust, her hips are jumping off the table. The vanity knocks against the wall over and over, creating a racket. It'd be obvious to any bystander what we're doing in here.

Between the building pleasure in my pelvis and the beautiful goddess in my arms, though, I don't give a shit. I don't give a shit if the whole audience is waiting outside the door, listening. "Say my name, baby."

"Grant..."

"Louder."

Her eyes jump into mine. Erotic terror trembling in her amber irises.

"*Louder,*" I demand, raising my voice as well.

"Grant...Grant...*Grant!*" On that last one, her head rolls back, and she lets out a strident cry. "Oh god, you're going to make me come!"

I go faster, as fast as I can until I see her face split in pleasure, her mouth falling open, eyes rolling back, almost a

look of pain. I can feel her pussy clenching around me. I don't stop. Not for me, though. I reach down between us and press my thumb against her clit.

"What are you doing?!" she cries out into my chest.

"Making you come again."

And as I continue thrusting into her, feeling electric pulses through my thighs, I work her clit with my thumb. Harder, harder, until–

"Oh, fuck, I'm coming," I curse into her hair, my last moment of sanity before I *fill her*. Just as she wanted.

Whether it's the force of my thumb or the warmth, Harley's body convulses as she comes again. Harder this time. She cries out something that isn't even words, curling herself into my chest and clutching my biceps weakly. "I can't–I can't–"

"Shhh...good girl," I whisper, idling my hips back and forth until I know I've been milked completely dry.

Harley lifts her head, a pained look on her face. "Not again, Grant."

I nod solemnly.

She swallows audibly and a look of determination settles on her face. "Never again."

THIRTEEN
HARLEY

I wake up the next morning in my bed with a horrid hangover. Dre and I partied practically all night after the awards ceremony. He kept asking me why I was in such a good mood. I didn't have it in me to tell him I'd gotten fucked backstage.

I wasn't sure if he asked too many questions if I wouldn't just break down and reveal the truth. I'd just fucked Grant Neville, otherwise known as my dad's best friend, backstage. For the second time.

And somehow it was even better than the first time.

I knew the second we got into that room alone that I was done for. I couldn't resist poking him just enough to see if he had been thinking of me.

And I hate to admit that when I realized he had been, my heart *sang* with the power of a choir of angels.

The space between my legs is sore in the best way. I rub my ankles together like a cricket and roll over in bed, a smile on my lips.

Fuck. Stop smiling, Harley. This is serious.

I need to tell someone. I can't keep going on like this. The guilt I'm feeling is twofold.

One, I've betrayed my father. Twice now. Three times and that's a pattern.

Two, I can't seem to stop betraying my father. In fact, the more I chastise myself, the more my mind gravitates toward Grant.

Two years ago, I promised myself *no more older men.* After all, what reason would a man nearly twice my age have to be with me? Unless something was wrong with him and he was looking to use me up?

However, from the way Grant worshipped my body last night, the commitment with which he made me come not once, but *twice,* well…

Most women would say to hold onto that man for dear life.

I throw the covers up and jump out of bed. I have to go see my dad. That will bring me back down to earth. Force me to repent my misgivings. I won't tell him, of course, that would be stupid and rash. It would just break his heart, and after everything, I can't do that to him.

I just need to be reminded of who I'm hurting. Then I can say the Grant Neville thing is done and dusted.

I HEAD over to Burbank after calling my dad and letting him know I'm going to drop by with coffee and pastries and he can't take no for an answer. Lucky for me, my dad is always, *always* prepared for a visit from one of his many daughters.

"You can help me pull weeds out of the garden!" he had said cheerfully.

"Dad, it's like ninety degrees," I say, lamenting the August heat.

I heard him laugh over the phone. "That's why I need my favorite weed-pulling daughter to help me." Then he hung up, not another word to be said.

I have donned my best weed-pulling attire (some old shorts and a tank top from a band that's no longer together) and head out on the highway on my hog. In the wake of my hangover, I take it easy and don't ride the middle line. And since I'm not wearing my usual leathers, I wear a helmet for Dana's sake.

I park down the block from Dad and hit up the coffee shop just a short walk away. He drinks scalding hot black coffee no matter the weather, whereas I'm an iced coffee girlie through and through. I'm also going to pick up some coffee cake because I've had a hankering for it.

As I stand in line, I can't help but wonder how Grant Neville takes his coffee. When I was interviewing him, he took it black with one sugar, but I can't help but think he was just trying to be polite. Dre would have happily run out and gotten him the most bougie, most specific latte his heart desired.

Maybe he's a cappuccino guy. Or Grant could just drink espresso. I never understood that. I need a whole drink to nurse throughout the morning, not just a little shot of coffee. I'm not doing shots at eight in the morning, even if it is caffeinated.

"Harley!"

My reverie is broken by a familiar voice. I look around the crowded café in confusion.

"Over here!"

It's Dana. I spot her over by the window sitting with...is that Drew? Former patient Drew? On a Sunday morning?

They're both wearing athletic gear, sweat dried on their faces. This isn't a joint walk of shame or just a friendly coffee. They went to exercise together. *Ew.*

I give her a wave.

"Come say hi once you've ordered!" she says with a grin.

"Yeah, okay, *mom.*"

She giggles and then returns to continue her conversation with Drew.

I order coffee for me and Dad and a whole coffee cake. I can't imagine just one piece is going to sate me. And if Dad has a piece and I have two pieces, I might as well just get a whole fucking coffee cake because...

Look, I don't need to defend myself.

After I collect my order, I walk over to Dana and Drew. "Hey, guys."

"Hey kid," Drew says.

"I resent that comment," I reply.

"Don't mind her," Dana says to Drew with a swipe of her hand. "Here, sit for a couple of minutes."

"I'm taking coffee to Dad, I need to–"

"He'll understand if you're saying hi to your sister for a minute. Come on, sit," Dana cajoles, pushing the third chair out with her foot.

I am about to push back on her one more time, but suddenly there's a pressing impulse inside me. I need to tell her. She's the only one of my sisters that will be able to listen without judgment. And as much as I'd like to think that seeing Dad will humble me, it also could be a fucking trainwreck. "Actually yeah, yeah, I'll sit for a few minutes." I settle into my chair and open the flat of coffee cake. "Want some?"

Dana eyes the coffee cake that's been split into six pieces. "Is that all for you and Dad?"

I grab a slice and take a big bite. "I like coffee cake, what about it?"

"I'll have a piece if you don't mind," Drew says with a sheepish smile.

"See? At least someone has taste. Be my guest, Drew."

Drew takes a piece of it out of the box as if he's an excited kid taking presents out of his stocking on Christmas morning.

"What are you two up to this morning?"

"We got up early and went for a run in Wildwood Canyon," Dana says.

I roll my eyes. "You two are weirdos."

"What did you do this morning?" she retorts. "Nurse a hangover in bed?"

Goddammit, how does she know me so well? "You don't gotta be rude about it."

She laughs.

"Dana says you were giving a presentation or...you were at a show last night," Drew says with a nervous look to Dana.

"An awards show. She was a presenter," Dana corrects. "How'd it go, Har?"

A genuine question that deserves a genuine answer. I'd love to give her a play-by-play. Tell her about how great I looked and all the compliments I got, not just on my outfit but on my work. I want to tell her about all the business cards I was able to exchange and how Dre and I had a fabulous time.

All that comes out is, "I fucked someone I shouldn't have."

Drew's mouth drops open revealing half chewed coffee

cake. Dana on the other hand, is unfazed. "Sorry, *who* did you fuck?"

I blink. "Um. Someone that I shouldn't have."

"Would this have anything to do with the weird one-night stand you had in the treehouse?" she asks with her eyebrow raised.

"You had sex with someone in a treehouse?" Drew asks, eyes bugging out.

"You'll catch up, Drew," I say with a half-smile.

Dana is still waiting for an answer.

"Might have something to do with that."

"And is the reason you shouldn't have fucked this person because he may or may not be Dad's best friend?"

My eyes bug out and Drew slaps a hand over his mouth to keep from asking another stupid question. "How the hell did you know that?"

"Because both of you were missing during the fireworks!" Dana shakes her head. "I can't believe this. I thought I was going crazy, but you really fucked–"

"Lower your voice!" I cry out in a whisper. "He's a public figure."

"You slept with a politician?!" Drew asks urgently. "Which one?"

"*Drew!*" Dana scolds him.

"I just want to know if I voted for him," he replies with a shrug.

I fold my hands over my eyes and lower my head. "Oh, my god. This is so embarrassing."

"Harley! Did you seriously have sex with Grant?"

I peek through my hands at my sister. She looks slightly disappointed in me. I close my eyes again. "Don't be mad at me."

"I'm not mad," Dana sighs. "Just...that's a lot to take in."

As I get the courage to pull my hands off my face, I hear Drew whisper, "Grant who?" to which Dana replies, "Grant Neville." She shushes him before he can repeat the name back in shock.

"I know, it was such a mistake."

"Such a mistake you did it twice," Dana mutters.

"You're not helping," I say, finally looking at her.

"Sorry, just..." She takes a deep breath and folds her hands. "No, you're right. I'm not being fair. Tell me about what happened."

And so the story unfurls from me. How at the party, things just got out of control. The attraction and the chemistry were just unignorable.

"We swore it would be a one-time thing, but then..."

"You had him on your radio show."

"That wasn't my fault!" I say. Which then leads me into explaining how Grant's PR person reached out to me about getting one of the artists from Infinium on the show. "And then I suggested Grant come on..." I say. "So, I guess it was kind of my fault."

"It was a good show, I don't think you should be upset," Drew says. Dana thwaps him on the arm.

I smile. "I didn't know you listened."

"Harley! Not the point right now!" Dana admonishes, getting me right back on track.

"Sorry! Okay!"

I dive back into the story, telling her about how amazing everything has been since the show. How people are asking for interviews and my show is finally getting meaningful national traction. All thanks to Grant.

"So then, I ran into him at the Auras last night and..." She doesn't need the whole play-by-play. "Things just...happened."

Dana sighs. "Oh dear, Harley."

"I know, it was so stupid and I knew we shouldn't, but we did and now I feel so guilty, Dana. I feel so guilty."

She smiles kindly. "I know you do."

"What do I do?"

"Well, what do you feel?"

"Uh, guilty. I just said tha—"

"Not that," she says with a shake of her head. "How do you feel about *Grant?*"

I furrow my brow. "Um..."

"Well, she either likes him or she's coping," Drew says. "Can I have another piece of coffee cake?"

"S-sure," I say, sliding the box his way. "I'm sorry, what did you say?"

Drew looks to Dana for permission to continue talking. "Go ahead. You are clearly hearing something I'm not," Dana says, leaning back in her chair.

"Well..." Drew swallows his latest mouthful of coffee cake. "The first time can be chalked up to just a chance meeting. Pheromones. Impulse. You know. A fling. But then you did it again. When you had an opportunity to step away and be rational. Which I think says something." Drew frowns and starts to gesticulate with his hands. "Clearly, you know that there is an element of danger here. And yet, you're pushing beyond that to satisfy some part of yourself. The question is...is that because you're not dealing with something perhaps painful that needs to be tended to so you're self-sabotaging? Or do you like him?"

"Wow, Drew, that was..." I trail off. His words have hit me like a ton of bricks. "Wow."

Dana smiles. "I've taught you well, grasshopper."

The three of us sit in silence as I sink into what Drew

has just said. "It would kill Dad if he found out," I say softly.

"Yeah. It would, probably. But that's not squarely on your shoulders. Grant was a part of this too."

I don't like how Dana uses the word "was" even though I know that's how it should be.

"But you know it would kill Dad even more if he knew you were shying away from something you thought would make you happy. Especially on his account."

Our eyes lock, matching amber blazing together.

"Damn. That's good, Dana," Drew says. "Can you believe I get this therapy for free?"

Dana glares at him playfully, "Yeah, maybe I need to start charging by the hour again." Then, back to me. "Just think about it, Harley. You know what to do. In your heart."

Her words stick with me long after I leave the café and well into weeding with Dad. He's so happy to see me that the guilt weighs heavier than ever on my mind. Thank god we don't spend long on pleasantries and coffee before he hustles me out to the garden to work on pulling out the overgrown weeds in the garden.

Dad fields questions my way about the awards show from the night before. I answer as plainly as I can, disinterested, chalking it up to my hangover, until he asks a question I can't ignore.

"Did you run into Grant?" he asks with a genuine innocent curiosity.

I pull out a nasty cloth of amaranth and throw it to the side. "Uh. No. Was he there?"

Dad guffaws. "I'm surprised you didn't see him!"

"No, I was kind of busy. You know. It all happened so fast."

He doesn't bat an eye. Clearly, he isn't suspecting

anything. "Well, I didn't know he was going. I was just looking at the press photos from the event last night and saw he was there with Victoria. I'm shocked you two didn't run into each other."

"Yeah. Me too," I reply. *Relax. Dad wants you to be happy. You did what made you happy.*

Yeah, that's a crock of shit.

"I just don't know how he does it. He's at an awards show one night and then jetting off to London the next morning at the crack of dawn."

I stop pulling weeds. "He's in London?"

"Oh yeah. Visiting the set of one of the new shows Infinium is producing. I think he's even doing some press. You might have just broken him out of his shell with that show of yours."

I smile to myself. Maybe that's why our paths needed to cross. We needed to walk each other into new phases of our lives. That would make all of this guilt worth something. Grant is onto greener pastures. And so am I.

And yet, just like the weeds return to infest the garden every year, I can't seem to shake the feeling that Grant and I aren't quite done.

FOURTEEN
GRANT

I'VE NEVER BEEN MORE STUNNED TO RECEIVE A TEXT message.

Usually, when a text comes through from an unfamiliar phone number, it's a phishing scam or some poor older woman whose thumb slipped when she was typing in the phone number.

It's never usually a woman I shouldn't have slept with. Twice.

> Hi, it's Harley. Heard you were in London.
> Say hi to Big Ben and Parliament for me. :)

I'm lying in bed with the covers pulled up to my chest. I was just about to clear out my inbox and pop a sleeping pill. Now my heart is pounding and sleep is *definitely* not in the cards for a while.

I've been in London for a week doing press and visiting our new studio. It's been a whirlwind meeting with talent, investors, and execs. And the interviews have been both welcoming and tedious. Ever since Harley and I sat down, I've found it more pleasant to talk about my work.

However, here in the UK, people are wondering why I deign to have Infinium compete with the likes of the BBC. The answer is because I can. The company is thriving, scandals notwithstanding. Why *not* try and compete with the BBC? I'm not a rash businessman, I know what I can handle. And this is the next step in total domination of entertainment on demand. Old intellectual properties from the UK are clamoring to be reinvigorated.

Harley's thoughts on the matter haven't left my brain. I know I'm sort of just...well, not even reinventing the wheel. And up until now, I've been able to push them away and justified that I'm doing what's best for the company and its longevity.

Now seeing her name on the screen makes me wonder if maybe I'm just scared of taking a risk.

The phone glows, her text message pulsing with potential. I could text her back. I could even call her. But maybe I should just ignore it.

Shit, I don't know.

We agreed nothing more should happen. And then we fucked again.

But that made sense in a perverse way. The first time we had sex was ushering in discomfort. And then the second time was ushering it out.

Too bad I'm still thinking about her every single freaking day.

Before I can decide what I'm going to do, I get another text.

> Shit, forgot it's the middle of the night there. Hope I didn't wake you up.

I chuckle. I am terrible at adjusting to jet lag. I've been here a week and my body clock is still a bit wonky.

Letting her know she didn't wake me up wouldn't hurt anyone. I wouldn't want her to feel bad. Listen to me justifying simply sending her a text...it's not like I'm inviting her over.

> No worries, can't sleep anyway. Good to hear from you :)

Sending a smiley face feels like age regression. Emoticons feel more suited to a younger generation. However, every now and then, it feels correct.

And I would like Harley to know that hearing from her put a smile on my face.

However, she doesn't reply. Her three dots appear on the screen and then nothing. I guess my text was a little final feeling. Good to hear from you, now fuck off.

That's not what I meant. Not at all. In fact, it's a very pleasant surprise.

I decide to follow up my text with a fairly innocuous question.

> How are things back in the States?

The three dots immediately return; my heart thumps as I wait...and wait...and wait.

God, is she typing a novel?

> Busy. Got a good interview coming out tomorrow. Hope you can tune in ;)

Not the wink. What the hell am I supposed to do with a wink when it makes my cock jump just thinking about her sultry little smile?

I drop the phone on my chest and look up at the ceiling of my hotel room. In the silence, I calculate the time difference. Her show is on at two pm Pacific time and in the UK it's Greenwich Mean Time. Except since it's summer, I think it's British Summer Time. That sounds fake. Whatever. I'm eight hours ahead.

So, it'll be around nine when her show airs.

Harley follows up with another text.

No pressure, I know you're busy.

If I can get Resa to move some things around, I should be free at nine.

Scratch that. I *will* be free at nine.

"HURRY, HURRY, HURRY!" I say, scrambling through the restaurant, dodging patrons and servers. "Pardon me, excuse me!"

"Grant, slow down! You don't have to do this in *heels*!"

I glance back at Resa. She is lagging behind. But we're closing in on nine o'clock. I can't be late. Not even by a second.

Once I get outside, I immediately spot the car, paying no mind to the paparazzi who are waiting outside the restaurant. I feel the heat of a few camera flashes before ducking into the black car. "Have you got it tuned, Arthur?"

"By the skin of my teeth," my driver, Arthur, responds in his cockney accent.

The satellite radio is tuned to WQXR and I can already hear the crunchy guitar of the *Someone's Gotta Do It* opening theme song. Skin of my teeth is right.

The door flies open and Resa throws herself inside.

"Remind me never to be chased by a pack of wolves with you," she grumbles.

"I'm sorry, this was…important."

"A little radio show is so important to you, huh?" she asks with a raised eyebrow.

I swallow. "I'm a fan, what can I say?"

"Yeah, clearly. Having me jumble your schedule all around just so you can tune in live. I don't think I've eaten dinner at five since I was a toddler."

"They cut things on the podcast version," I explain with finality, hoping she'll shut up so I can listen. I do owe Resa a lot of favors. Or a nice bonus. She moved up our dinner and drinks with a couple of UK producers. They love to hear themselves talk so we had to really move up the start time.

"Hotel?" Arthur asks.

"No, no. Just drive," I say, waving a hand toward Arthur.

"*I'm* going to the hotel," Resa says sternly.

"Fine. Drop her off and then just drive me, alright?"

As soon as Harley's voice comes through the speakers, the rest of the world falls away. "Hi, I'm Harley Solace coming to you live on WQXR and this is *Someone's Gotta Do It*, where I come to you five days a week to pull back the curtain on careers across sector boundaries to show you just how hard America is working.

"This week's guest has been one you've been clamoring for. I'm so excited to introduce Elma Holland who has been a ranger at Yosemite National Park for over thirty years. Thanks for joining us this week, Elma."

"That's what people were clamoring for? A park ranger?" Resa asks with a sneer.

"*Shhh!* You don't get it," I reply.

She laughs. "Okay, okay."

I listen with rapt attention the whole way back to the hotel. Resa waits until a commercial break in order to speak to me. "You really are obsessed with this girl, huh?"

My eyebrows leap. "Huh?!"

"This podcast. You think it's special or something, right?"

Yes. The podcast. Not the girl. Definitely not. "Yeah, there's something really special about it."

"*This American Life* with a female Ira Glass."

"That's reductive," I say as a jangly commercial for some law firm in LA plays.

Resa chuckles, "You know what I mean. Have you ever thought of doing something with her?"

She couldn't possibly know what's happened between Harley and me, but the way she's talking is making it painfully difficult to assume otherwise. "What do you mean?"

"I don't know. A docuseries or maybe something where she's a host. If you think it has potential, think about it."

I don't have time to respond before the intro music starts again.

"Okay, I'm out. Enjoy your show, boys."

"Thank you, ma'am," Arthur nods.

Resa steps out of the car hurriedly and heads inside the hotel, leaving me with Arthur and the sweet voice of Harley Solace.

"Just drive, sir?"

I lean back in my seat. "Yeah. Just drive."

I LISTEN to the whole hour-long show in the car with Arthur and we talk about the show for another half hour afterward. It's nice to have someone to chat with about the show and all our thoughts and feelings about being a park ranger in the US. I guess Harley's show is doing exactly what she set out to do–bringing people together.

Once I'm back in my hotel room, though, there's someone else I'd like to talk to about the show. Harley herself.

But I don't just want to play the young man's game of texting. It's silly and fruitless.

No, I think I'm much more interested in hearing her voice. Even if it is thousands of miles away.

I don't think about it long enough to actually consider the repercussions. She must have just finished up, is still at work, probably moving on to the next part of her day.

But who can refuse a call from Grant Neville?

I press the call button and pull a bottle of wine out of the fridge. One ring and then–

"Did you listen?"

Her voice isn't as clear as it is on the radio. But it's just for me this time. "I did. It was a fantastic episode. As usual."

"Well, thank you."

I grab a corkscrew and twist it into the bottle. "Have a drink with me?"

"It's not even four here."

"Well, it's almost eleven here and I'm having a glass of wine before bed. Catch up."

Harley laughs. "I'll have coffee, how's that?"

"Perfect."

I hear her take a careful sip over the phone as I pour a nice, Italian red into a glass. "So, a park ranger is one of your most sought-after guests?"

"Oh, yes, you should see the tweets I get."

I pick up my phone and glass of wine and go over to the

bed. "Well, I think you did a masterful job considering how rambly Elma seems to get."

"You know, it takes all kinds," she replies. "I don't mind. Better than having someone who only gives one-word answers."

I settle into bed, into the plush pillows, unable to ignore the thought I'd like her to be lying right in bed next to me telling me about her day. "Who has been your worst interview?"

"Grant, I can't answer that. I'm at the office. All my interviews are my favorite interviews."

I sip my wine and stretch out. "Just tell them you're talking to me. Business. Take the rest of the day off and hide in a conference room. Talk to me."

I hope I don't sound desperate. But god, it would be nice to have someone to talk to. Especially someone with a sweet voice perfect for radio. With a face for television.

Harley hesitates and then, to my relief, answers, "Alright. Give me two minutes."

And two minutes later, we're shooting the shit, laughing, and catching up on the week since we've seen each other.

A terrible thought dawns on me halfway through our call. I could get really used to this. I know I should stop before it becomes a habit.

But fuck it. I'm not going to miss out on what I want. Not anymore.

FIFTEEN
HARLEY

"I should let you go," I whisper.

"No...don't," Grant replies, his voice laden with exhaustion.

I giggle and prop my feet up on my balcony railing. It's a gorgeous Saturday and I'm spending it doing *nothing*.

Except talking to my new best friend, Grant Neville. Am I allowed to call him a best friend if we've fucked twice and he's also my *dad's* best friend?

Since I texted him a week ago, we've been talking every single day. Or night for him. They almost feel like little dates, except for the fact we're on different continents. But I love being the last voice Grant hears at night. Makes me feel special.

Especially since he keeps coming back.

"I can keep talking," Grant continues adamantly.

"Grant, you've got an early flight. Just rest."

He grumbles something under his breath.

"What was that?"

"Nothing, I just..." He sighs. "Once I'm back in LA there's no reason to talk on the phone anymore."

My lips curl to the side. "You like talking to me?"

"Jee, is it obvious?"

I giggle and take a sip of my cold brew. "I like talking to you too, Grant."

"God, how old are we?"

"*We* might have very different answers for that."

"Don't remind me."

While our age difference is part of the reason I tried to stay away, it's also one of the things I like about talking with him. He's mature and grounded. Meanwhile, I'm young and feel like I have my head in the clouds.

I definitely do when it comes to him. "There won't be a reason to talk on the phone anymore because you'll be back in LA, and you can see me in person."

Grant goes quiet. Shit, have I said the wrong thing?

"Only...if you want." My stomach flips. At first, I think it's from nerves, but then I feel a wave of nausea hit me all of a sudden.

"I want to, Harley. You know I do. But–"

I press my hand to my mouth.

"You know it's complicated."

"Y-yeah," I force a response through the feeling. "Totally complicated."

Grant takes a breath. "Let's both think about it."

I nod, though he can't see me.

"Alright?"

"Yes! Yeah, sorry I'm–" What's wrong with me? "I have to go, I'll–" Maybe I won't talk to him later. "Bye."

"B–"

I hang up before he can even respond, bounding through the sliding glass door of my apartment to the kitchen sink. I brace myself against the stainless steel and hurl my guts into the sink. I haven't had much to eat today, so the acidic coffee burns my throat. "Fuck..." I curse, spitting out what's left of the vomit coating my mouth.

The smell is putrid and all I can do is thank god I only had coffee or I'd need a garbage disposal as I wash the upchuck down the drain.

I need to eat something. A piece of toast. Some buttered pasta. Chicken soup. Something neutral to settle my stomach.

Hopefully, that'll fix everything.

For a second, my mind goes to Grant. Despite just emptying my stomach, I feel like there are still rocks rolling around in there. Every one of our phone calls, no matter how they end, has made me feel sick to my stomach.

They've never made me *actually* sick.

Unless...

No. I'm not going to think like that. There's no way I could be pregnant. Okay. Not *no* way, but...

One bout of nausea doesn't mean anything. And that's the story I'm sticking to.

THE NEXT DAY, the nausea comes again. And two bouts of nausea make things harder to ignore. It's clear to me that it's not a stomach bug. There are no other symptoms. Just bouts of vomiting and then...I'm normal. Except for my increased hankering for coffee cakes. And...if I'm honest with myself, my breasts are kind of tender.

I'm willing to wait for a third bout to establish a pattern, but that all changes when I get a text from Grant about midway through my Sunday.

Just landed. I want to see you.

And there's no way I can see him and not know *for sure* that I'm not...*pregnant.*

God, just thinking the word makes me lightheaded.

So, I make an emergency appointment with my gyno. I'm lucky she's just had an opening tomorrow morning, bright and early. I'll take the first half of the day off, pray that I'm overreacting, and then head into work to interview my latest subject.

Scratch that, that isn't going to work. I'll have to get Dre to cover for me in case I'm in full crisis. He's done it once before when I came down with a nasty bout of bronchitis. He can do it again.

Hopefully, that will just be the price of my peace of mind.

———

"How do you want to proceed, Harley?"

She may as well have not said anything. Because the rest of the world is tuned out, replaying the words she's just said to me on repeat.

"Your urine sample came back positive. You're pregnant."

Twenty-six is hardly too young to have a baby, but I feel like I've just started to lay down roots and grow again after all my time in Australia.

Not to mention the father. Dear god, *the father* of my baby...is my father's best friend and nearly twice my age.

The father of my baby is Grant Neville.

I've always played it a little bit fast and loose. Risk keeps it fun.

And now, all of that playing has come to bite me in the ass.

"Harley?"

"I don't–" I shoot my head up to look at her. "I don't know."

Dr. Freeman smiles at me gently. "That's okay. It's a big decision." She looks down at her chart. "Your hCG levels still suggest things are early. You have time to rest and think about it."

I take a deep breath. "Thanks." My voice cracks. And suddenly, tears are streaming down my face.

"Oh, honey, it's okay. Here, take my hand."

I take Dr. Freeman's hand as she consoles me. She's no stranger to that. One time I thought I had an ovarian cyst that turned out to be really bad gas and she really supported me through that even though I was being a bit dramatic.

"You are totally in charge of this. It's your body," Dr. Freeman coos.

I can't let her know that's not the reason I'm crying. It's not that I'm completely confused and need to go sleep on the idea of becoming a mother, probably a single mother since there's no way anyone can ever know I slept with Grant Neville unless I want to be eaten alive by my sisters (and I know Dana will keep my secret; she's good about that).

No, the reason I'm crying is because I know. I know the answer so well it scares me.

I want this baby. I can't wait to have this baby.

I just wish I could share it with the man who gave it to me. A man I've implicitly cared about my whole life and now, in a short month and a half, yearn for with such intensity I feel like I might break in two. A baby only makes sense as the culmination of that fire.

Dr. Freeman sits with me until I've shed my tears and then walks me through what I should do next. Prenatals, checkups, etcetera. I take notes on my phone with immense detail, wiping my tear-stained cheeks and nodding along with what she says.

When I leave and head out to my car, the Los Angeles sunshine beats down on me. August. *Hot.* Somehow my body is covered in goosebumps. I'm freezing cold, stomach sinking.

Pregnant.

And yet, I can't help the smile that slips onto my face.

I've always been a person who loves adventure. I'm just now realizing my definition of the word has been too narrow. Adventure isn't just riding my bike up the California coast with no destination in mind. Having a baby is going to be an adventure in and of itself. The best one, hopefully.

It's also one I know I won't be able to do alone or quietly for that matter. I'm not ready to spill my guts to my sisters or my dad, yet my body aches to be around them. Just for comfort.

So, I hop on my bike (helmet on this time—got to think about getting something a bit more *sensible* for the immediate future) and head out to Burbank. Dad will be home. He still works at the law firm but only three days a week. He's so close to retirement. Then he can spend a lot of time in his garden.

I feel like a new woman as the air whips around me. My heart beats with anticipation and my mind swirls with questions.

How am I going to pull this off? I can't imagine Grant is interested in having a baby under these circumstances. But can I lie to my family? Tell them it was just a mistake, a roll in the hay. Just like Gillian....I've always given her so much shit. Not really for *that*, but...

Maybe we're more alike than I'd like to acknowledge.

I get to the house and let myself in with my house keys. "Dad! Are you home?" I call out. I didn't check the garage for his car. "I took the day off from work. Thought we could grab some lunch or I could help around the house or–"

I stop dead in my tracks when I walk into the living room and see a very familiar face.

A face so familiar it may as well be mine when I look in the mirror.

"Mom?"

My mother is sitting on a couch in the living room. She looks at me with her sparkling brown eyes and a smile appears on her face. It feels forced. She didn't expect me to just waltz in unannounced. "Harley? Is that–" She gets to her feet. "Is that really you?"

I'm transported back in time, looking at my mom in the house I grew up in. Just as it should have always been. Except she fucked it up.

"What are you doing here?" I ask in a small voice.

Mom takes a few steps toward me but notices my retreat. "I came back."

"Why?"

"I wanted to see you and your sisters and..." She presses her hands to her mouth in a prayer position. "It's been so long."

Over ten years ago, this woman walked out of my life. Why would she want to see us now instead of when any of us graduated high school or when Gillian had a baby or when Amy got a book deal or...There are so many *whys* floating around in my head.

My dad appears in the doorway to the kitchen with two cups of coffee, one for each of them. He looks as if he's seen a ghost, and he may as well have.

"Did you know she was coming?" I ask him, pointing at my mother as if she's a scientific specimen.

Dad shakes his head slowly. "N-no."

"It was a spur-of-the-moment decision," Mom says with a laugh. "Let me hug you, Harley. Please, let me..."

I tighten my whole body as she loops her arms around me. But the second I smell her perfume, I lose my composure. So many memories flooding back. I forget the whys and the how comes. All I can do is curl into my mother's chest, weeping for all the lost years.

"I'm so sorry, Harley. I'm here now."

I don't even care why she's here or what she really wants.

Because what I need right now more than anything is a mom.

SIXTEEN

GRANT

I harden my gaze on Victoria's mimosa, watching the champagne bubbles trembling in the glass. She's going on and on about her latest job. Normally, I'm a good listener, but I'm distracted.

I haven't heard from Harley. I landed yesterday and texted her right when we landed before the seatbelt sign was off. Yet...nothing.

I can't say I'm surprised considering we were both acting strange at the end of our last phone call. Although we *always* act strange at the end of our phone calls. God, I say that as if it's a habit we've been in for months, not just a week.

While in London, I spent hours on the phone with Harley, somehow getting by on just a few hours of sleep each night in order to accommodate her work schedule. If that doesn't mean I got it bad for her, I don't know what does.

It was just so...easy. The back and forth, the rapport. It was hard to break the flow of our conversations. And, while I tried to remain on my best behavior, I couldn't help throwing in a flirtation every now and then. Nothing crude, of course. No "What are you wearing?" or anything like that. Just little things to let her know I admire her. Which I do. With every fiber of my being. Mind, body, soul.

Harley Solace has totally enchanted me.

"...I don't know, I think I need to talk to my lawyer about the contract," Victoria says, picking under one of her long, manicured nails. "It might be Dior, but it's practically slave labor."

That joke is enough to get me back on track. Except for the night of the awards, I haven't seen my sister in nearly a month, what with her traveling around the world for photo-shoots and preparing for fashion week and me on my own hectic schedule. She deserves my undivided attention.

And yet, underneath it all, my heart burns for Harley.

"Fuck Dior," I say. "You don't need them."

Victoria smiles and giggles, leaning on her elbows. We might be two of the most notable people in the world, but our upbringing still shines through. Elbows on the table and everything. "Well, we'll see. I think I look really nice in the commercials. In fact, I actually had someone reach out to me through my agent who might be *interested* in me, if you catch my drift."

"Vic, that's great!"

She laughs. "When you hear who it is, you'll be singing a different tune."

I narrow my eyes, trying to imagine who it could be when it dons on me. "Oh *no*."

"Flick—"

"*Oh no.*"

"—Harrison."

I slam my fist on the table. The silverware clatters.

"Grant, please! It's not that serious."

"I didn't mean for it to be that dramatic, I just–" I take a deep breath. "Flick Harrison might be the stupidest man on the planet. Doesn't he get how last names work?"

Victoria shrugs. "Honestly, he just seems like the type of man who thinks with his dick. He probably saw a picture of me and doesn't even know my last name."

"You're literally the biggest supermodel of the–"

She holds up her hand to stop me. "It doesn't matter, Grant. It never matters with those kinds of guys."

I sigh. Having a sister is full of moments like this. Seeing how genuinely unfairly women are treated, always wishing I could fight to make things better, knowing that she's become so used to being treated like an object and resigned to that never changing. Lucky for me, Victoria has grown to be strong. Her "fuck you" attitude keeps her safe.

Still, though. I wish I could do more.

"I'm going to talk to him," I say with a sigh.

"I'm not telling you this for you to get mad on my account, Grant. I'm telling you because it's probably a *fact* that he's reaching out to other women besides me."

"Of course."

"I just have a vested interest in your success to keep it from the press."

I smirk sadly. "Has nothing to do with me being your brother?"

Victoria sips her mimosa. "Not at all."

I laugh but am interrupted by my phone buzzing in my pocket. My mind immediately goes to Harley. "Sorry, I need to check this," I say to Victoria as I fish my phone out of my pocket.

"Take your time."

To my disappointment, Harley's name is not on the screen. And to my curiosity, I don't *know* who is calling.

Whomever it is has blocked their number. I know in most circumstances to leave things like this alone. It's probably a spam caller or, on the rare occasion, a crazy who has managed to get my number and wants to pitch me some god-awful television show.

For some reason, though, I can't just leave it alone this time. I pick up the call and press the phone to my ear. "Hello?"

"Grant Neville. How're you doing, old friend?"

My heart drops into my stomach. It's been years since I've heard the voice and yet it feels like just yesterday.

"You haven't forgotten about me, have you?"

I swallow. "No, of course not. How are you, Malcolm?"

Victoria looks up from her phone screen, eyes wide.

I can't do this call with her listening in. I get up and walk toward the back of the restaurant, onto their patio, which is only half full due to the heat.

"Well, mostly good. Been better, though."

"Been better, huh? Find that hard to believe since you've got Aileen wrapped around your finger."

"Grant, don't be like that."

"I'll be however I like." Since stealing our best friend's wife out from under his nose, I don't think Malcolm Jenkins deserves one drop of sympathy, regardless of the situation.

Malcolm sighs. "I thought you might be happy to hear from me. After all, it's been over ten years."

"Not long enough." Or too long. Not sure.

"I guess you and Kent are done with me, huh?"

I grit my teeth. "Let's not get the facts twisted. *You* were done with *us*. Don't act like we did away with you because you–"

"Whoa, whoa, whoa. Grant, *relax*."

I listen, only because I'm in public. If I was somewhere

private, I'd berate him even further. If he was in front of me, in the flesh, I might even grab him by the collar. *Don't you fucking tell me to relax.*

"Listen, I'm not a perfect person. Who is?"

"A lot of people abstain from fucking their friends' wives," I mumble.

"You're still all bent out of shape about that, huh? Carrying the torch for Kent? Listen, I've tried to apologize. He would never listen."

I'm not sure I believe him.

"Plus, you know, it takes two to tango. Aileen wasn't the most innocent of characters when it really comes down to it."

I hate that he's right. Aileen really was the wolf in sheep's clothing in all of this. Malcolm had been a womanizer from day one. Aileen had the perfect cover. A loving mother and wife. I don't blame her more than him, but she isn't without fault, that's for damn sure. "How is she?"

"You'll be happy to know she's doing very well enjoying the LA sunshine."

The LA sunshine...?

"In fact, we both are. We just got into town last night. We have people we need to see,"

"You're telling me she's gone to see Kent?"

"And the girls, of course."

Dear god. Harley. I can't imagine that this is at all welcome. In fact, from everything I've learned just over the past week, I know she still nurses the hurt of her mother's abandonment every day. "And you?"

"Oh, Grant. I thought it was obvious."

I raise an eyebrow. How could any of this be obvious when he calls me from an unknown phone number out of the blue and drops all this information on me? How could I possibly connect the dots?

"I'm here to see you."

The muscles in my neck tense up. I have no way of responding to him.

"Because we have quite a bit of unfinished business."

"Do we, now?"

I can practically hear his evil grin through the phone. *Bastard.* "I gave you seed money," he says.

"Seed money? For what? " I reply and begin pacing back and forth.

"Don't play dumb, Grant."

I'm not. I have no idea what he's talking about.

"I gave you the startup money for Infinium."

I snort, thinking he might be joking. "Emphasis on the word *gave*, Malcolm."

"Grant, we're businessmen. Nothing is ever free."

He can't be serious.

"Your company exists almost solely because of me. I've never seen any return on my investment."

I can't believe my ears. "It was a gift."

"*Seed money* is an investment, Grant."

"Malcolm–" I try to rewind time, back to the moment he offered. The kindness in his eyes. The light. Kent and I both know now what a good liar he was. But he couldn't have possibly planned a con as long as this, could he? Tell his friend he was giving him money as a gesture of good faith only to turn the tables and claim ownership of my empire? "It was a gift. Don't you remember? We were sitting by the pool at Kent's house. We were drinking–" I started laughing at how ridiculous it all was. "We were drinking Mike's Hard Lemonade. And the girls were all swimming in the pool with Kent while Aileen was tending toward a skinned knee. And *you* brought it up."

"So what if *I* brought it up?"

"I didn't *ask* you for investment money. You offered it. In good faith." Not that Malcolm would know what those words mean. After all, he was fucking his best friend's wife for years and then stole her away, never to be heard from again. He's selfish. And doesn't have a faithful bone in his body.

"I never said that."

"You didn't say anything other than 'Let me make it easier for you,'" I reply quickly. I can remember the whole interaction word for word.

Malcolm pauses and then says, "Well, I'm not sure anecdotal evidence will hold up in court."

"Court? You're...you're suing me?"

"Bingo. You were always the smart one, Grant."

"What does that make you?" I ask, jaw tense. "If *I* was the smart one."

He laughs. "Well, you were smart, I was charming, and Kent...well..." There's a pitiful tone in his voice that I don't like. "He's a good guy. He really is."

"If he's good, you're—"

"Let's not start name-calling or anything, eh?" Malcolm interrupts. "Listen, I have the request drafted. All you have to do is fulfill it. Otherwise, lawyer up, buttercup."

"You've got a lot of nerve to—"

"Don't say that like you're surprised. I've always taken what I wanted. Always. Why should this be any different?"

I look around and suddenly realize people are watching me. I guess I am a recognizable face. Hopefully, none of them heard me talking about being sued. That's the last thing I need TMZ commenting on.

Okay, maybe not the last. But it's definitely on the list.

"Listen, I gotta go. We'll talk, 'kay?"

"Why in the world would I waste my breath on you?"

Malcolm pauses. "I'd think long and hard about how you want to proceed, Grant. You know how shrewd I am."

"Malcolm, it's been over ten years. I don't know anything about you."

"Hmm. Guess you're right. Well. Ciao."

The call goes dead. I stand there, the Los Angeles sun beating down on me. I want to scream out a string of curse words but hold it in. People are always watching in LA.

I don't know Malcolm anymore. I don't know how conniving or cutthroat he's become. This could be dangerous.

But he also doesn't know who *I've* become and what I'm capable of.

I'm Grant Fucking Neville. I get what *I* want. I'm just not a fucking heartless piece of shit about it.

SEVENTEEN
HARLEY

It feels like a fever dream, sitting in the living room of my childhood home with my mother, a woman I never thought I'd see again in my life. And if I did, I imagined it would be on her deathbed as she attempted to make amends before she met her maker.

Instead, it's the day I've found out I'm pregnant with Dad's best friend's baby. As if I wasn't already thinking about all the betrayal my dad has gone through in his life, then *she* shows her face.

I'm sitting next to Amy who walked in shortly after I did; she has been doing her drawing in a park nearby in order to avoid the new neighbor's annoying habits. It was interesting to see how the shock transpired through her versus how I felt it through me. Mine came in a wave, crashing over me, emotion tumbling outward. Unusual for me...although not so unusual now that I know my emotions are about to be haywire for eight more months and then some.

Amy, on the other hand, was frozen in time, her expression of concern not dropping from her face, even when she conceded to a hug from Mom.

"You were so little the last time I saw you," Mom had said as she wrapped Amy in an embrace.

Amy was fourteen at the time and did have a ginormous growth spurt in high school. But Mom is acting like she left babies behind when we were girls about to grow into young women. Hell, Dana was already out of high school.

For Dad's sake, Amy and I are keeping our cool. I can't even imagine how he is feeling. He's trying to be sweet, his quintessential Kent Solace way. With his delicate voice and smile, you wouldn't know he's a high-powered entertainment lawyer. He was always meant to be a girl dad.

I don't know how Mom could have given up such a good man. Many women have tried to take her place, but Dad has never been on a date since she left. At least as far as I know.

"I know you're wondering why I'm here," Mom says, speaking to Amy and me as if we're little kids about to be told Santa isn't real. "All of you," she says with a look toward Dad.

Judging by the ring on her left ring finger, I know this isn't some attempt at getting the family back together. I'm sure as soon as the dust settled from the divorce, Malcolm and Mom got married. It breaks my heart that she left Dad, and, for some other perverse reason, it breaks my heart I didn't get to see her get married again.

I would have taken any amount of Mom over none at all. Even if she's a traitor.

"I want...to patch things up," Mom says with a weak smile.

Out of the corner of my eye, Dad visibly winces.

"I know that things between you and me are forever altered, Kent. I took that risk and I know I need to pay for that for...well, as long as you would like me to," she says to Dad.

"I feel like you should know that you're going to be atoning for that as long as you live," Amy pipes up with a sassy cock of her head.

"*Amy*," Dad scolds.

"What?! She's–" Amy stops speaking when Dad looks at her just a bit harder. He has never wanted us to fight his fight for him. After all, we have our own grudges against our mother. I can only imagine the shame that he's felt over the years of being abandoned by our mother. Perhaps he thinks we see him as less of a man. That couldn't be farther from the truth.

But none of this has ever made sense.

"It's alright," Mom says. She dares to reach out and touch Dad on the knee. *Tenderly*. The way they used to. A fire alights inside me. How dare she touch him like that? "I know they have an allegiance to you. How could they not after everything I've done?" She looks back to Amy and me. "All I'm asking for is a chance."

"To do what?" I ask. I might have hugged her and enjoyed her embrace. But she's no longer the mom who used to tend to me in the middle of the night after a bad dream or the one I would look for at school pickup.

She abandoned us. I can never trust her again.

"Well, to get to know you all again. Maybe even be in your lives." Mom swallows, the diamond necklace on her neck shifting against her collarbone. Damn, Dad always did well for us, but Malcolm must be swimming in it. "I know Gillian has a daughter of her own now."

I feel a tickling in the pit of my stomach. I might have my own soon as well.

"And you write books for children," she says to Amy

with a beaming, proud smile. "You're on the radio, Harley. And..." She trails off. "I know I haven't been in touch, but I've never been very far. I've always kept my eye on you."

"The least you could do..." Amy says under her breath.

I glance at Dad. He's hidden his face in his hand, leaning on the arm of his chair. He's learned how to be a covert crier over the years, hiding his heartbreak from all of us girls whenever he can. I can't imagine how he feels right now. "How do you suppose we go about getting to know each other again?" I ask, more vitriol in my voice than intended.

"Well...I know it will take a while, but–"

"Are you living in LA now? Because I think to undo the years of damage you've done, it might take longer than a two-week vacation to Malibu."

"Harley..." Dad warns, but he doesn't have the strength like he did earlier. He's waning.

"I'm sorry, Dad, but I'm not going to sit here and let these platitudes somehow make up for the past ten years." I stare at my mother with laser-beam focus. "Ten years you've been gone. Not so much as a word or a phone call."

Mom's eyebrows jump.

"How can you possibly make up for that now?"

"Harley, *please*, don't make this–" Dad tries to tame me again, but Mom intercedes quickly.

"She's always been the outspoken one. I expected this," she says with...is that a smile? "Harley, you might not know the power of shame quite yet, but–"

"I'm a grown-ass woman. Don't tell me I don't know the power of shame." This is my interview with Grant all over again. Being infantilized and condescended to. What is it about me that makes people believe I've had it so easy in my life? Why do people assume I haven't been hurt? "I know how it can eat you from the inside out." *Just like my relationship with Grant and this unplanned pregnancy is doing right now.* "That's not a good enough reason not to speak to *your children.*" My voice wavers at the end there. It's too much.

My mother's face screws together tightly. No amount of Botox can hide how my words have stabbed her in the gut. "I've made mistakes, Harley. I didn't handle things as well as I should have back then. Haven't handled them well in the past ten years. If it takes ten years or more for me to patch things up, well…" She throws up her hands and slaps them against her thighs. "That's what I'll do."

Amy reaches for my hand and squeezes it. We're thinking the same thing. I just know it.

Something here just isn't right. Why *now?*

That's an answer we're going to have to find out the hard way. And that means…letting Mom back in.

"Girls," Dad suddenly speaks. His eyes are rimmed with red as he leans forward in our direction. I can't imagine how painful this must be. I know his love for her has never faded. Or should I say the love he had for the woman he thought she was? "I know this hurts. I know it does. But can we…" He puts his hand on his chest. "Can we just try to hear her out?"

What he doesn't say is, "Can you do it for me?" I hear it anyway, though. And my actions in the past month and change might not indicate it, but I would do anything for my dad.

Except resist his best friend, apparently.

I look between my parents, one of whom I love with everything I have in me and the other I wish would go back to where she came from. And I decide in that moment that everything with Grant has to go away. He will only be a part of my life insofar as my father brings him around.

There is no way I am going to be a traitor to my father like my mother was. I'm not going to let him lose another friend.

The baby will be mine and mine alone. And we will both be better off for it. After all, it's quite obvious to me looking at my parents, who I thought were the perfect couple up until the very night my life completely changed, that all love is a lie. You can't count on it.

My baby will be able to count on my love. And my love alone.

I guarantee it.

Amy looks at me, waiting for me to speak. We might be the two youngest Solace girls, but I'm the older one of the two. It's my job to protect her. "I think before we do anything else, we need to get Gillian, Kira, and Dana here as soon as possible." I turn my attention back to my mother, zeroing my amber eyes into hers. "Then we can talk."

She manages to smile elegantly in return. Not in thanks.

But in victory.

I haven't had a moment's rest since Malcolm called me.

After I hung up the phone, I cut my lunch short with Victoria and headed straight to the office to meet with my lawyers. Malcolm's lawyers beat me to the punch. Damage control was already underway.

I didn't leave the office until two in the morning.

Now, I'm lying in bed running through everything in my head.

It's true, he did give me money to start Infinium. I'd just had a failed business venture that came crashing down right around the time Netflix took root as a digital platform, completely making physical media obsolete.

I was broken, bereft, tired of asking strangers to believe in me when I didn't believe in myself.

And that's when my friend, or a man I thought was my friend, gave me the courage I needed to start again. Malcolm's own investments were thriving. He had an expendable income and *then* some. Out of the three of us, he was living a life of luxury. Didn't know what to do with all his money.

"Just a token of my gratitude for our years of friendship," he'd said with a wink.

Now, he's gone and changed the narrative.

I guess I should have known that his money came at a price. Why was I so naïve?

Ever since our phone call, things have spiraled. Malcolm is coming for me.

He's coming for Infinium. The only thing I have. The thing I've slaved over for all these years, foregone so many of my personal relationships to build. Maybe I could have fallen in love and started a family instead of lusting after Harley.

Who am I kidding? That wouldn't have happened regardless. I'm too...fucked up for that.

My tossing and turning is cut short when my phone buzzes on the nightstand.

Aileen came home.

Fuck. I should have warned him. But I was too caught up with Infinium...I'm a shit friend if that weren't already clear.

I don't know what to do.

God, my poor friend. Poor *us.* I respond quickly with my own drama, hoping it might balance things out.

Malcolm wants Infinium.

He wants to destroy me. After he's already destroyed so much.

I don't know if I've ever met anyone more selfish in my life.

A few seconds later, Kent sends back a simple

...

My friend needs me. That much is clear.

Come by at noon for lunch. We'll talk.

When Kent arrives at my office, he looks like an absolute wreck. It's like he's gone gray overnight. I don't think I've ever seen him unshaven in my life. He looks at the roomful of lawyers and looks like he might shrink into his suit jacket and disappear.

"Hey," I say, standing from my desk.

"Hey," he replies, forcing his hands into his pockets.

I scan the room and then wave my hand. "Clear the room."

The lawyers, all of whom have been working overtime since yesterday afternoon, skitter away like marbles in a ring until Kent and I are the only ones left in my office.

Thirty years. We've known each other for thirty years. *Over* thirty years if we want to be exact about it. Even though he looks a mess, I still see the eighteen-year-old guy playing pool in the frat house with a carefree smile. Little did he know then what we'd be up against today.

I go to my friend and wrap my arms around him. We hug tightly. We're not the most touchy-feely people, but we are when it counts. And both of us need this more than anything.

"God, what am I going to do?" Kent wails into my chest.

"It's okay," I say, patting his back. "It's…"

It all flashes through my mind at once. I've been a traitor. I've been callous and underhanded, pursuing his daughter, pretending I can't hold myself back.

What the fuck kind of man can't hold himself back? Can't control himself? Harley might be the most beautiful woman on earth. She may be making me have feelings I haven't had in years. And I might want her with every fiber of my being.

But it's wrong. I can't cross the line again.

If Kent ever found out, it would ruin him. I know it would. I could do my best to keep it under wraps, pray no one would ever catch on. But even the thought of that disgusts me. It makes me sound like Malcolm.

Although, unlike Malcolm, I'd never revel in Kent's pain.

"Come on. Sit down," I say, wrapping my arm around his shoulder and leading him to the sitting area in my office. "Let's order some food and talk."

Kent sniffles and collapses onto the couch. He rubs his face. "I don't know, Grant. I don't know."

"Let me get you some water." We might both be suffering, but he's had to come face to face with his ex-wife, the mother of his children. The woman he thought he'd grow old with. I thought that too. They seemed to be made for each other from the moment they met. In fact, they were married with Dana on the way before graduation. I thought they were crazy, and yet it made complete sense.

Then, she destroyed so many years of happy memories with her selfishness. Only to show up a decade later to tear the wound open again.

I pour him a glass and hand it to him. Kent chugs it almost in its entirety. "God, do you have anything stronger?" he asks.

I chuckle. "I have them bringing something up with lunch."

He sighs. "Perfect."

"You've been through it," I say as I sit in the chair closest to the couch.

"You have too, apparently."

I wave my hand toward him. "We're not talking about me. You first."

"God, it was just awful. She showed up at the house

and then Harley and Amy came home within ten minutes and–"

As he babbles, I imagine the horror in Harley's eyes when she saw her mother again for the first time. I hate that I wish I could reach out and speak to her. Hold her in my arms. Comfort her.

Good lord...letting her go is going to be hell.

"It's so fucked up, Grant," Kent mutters, his knee bouncing. "I'm so fucked up."

"No, you're not."

"I *am*," he says firmly. "I'm–I'm so screwed up. Because...because..." He looks up at me, eyes glossy. "Grant, when I saw her at the door, I felt like I used to."

Oh no.

"It has never gone away. Ten fucking years and I still–" He closes his eyes. "*Love her.*"

The way his voice comes out, strangled and pained. It breaks my heart. "It's only natural, Kent."

"No, it's not. She betrayed me. She left me and our children and–"

"Exactly. Your children, Kent. She's the mother of your girls. Of course, you still love her."

Kent shakes his head. "I've imagined this day. I've..." He chuckles sadly. "I've dreamed about it. Her coming back to me. But this isn't what that is, is it?"

With Malcolm back in the picture, no, definitely not.

"She has a wedding ring now. They're fucking married," he says and kicks the coffee table.

"Easy, Kent. Easy." I can't imagine how complicated this must feel for him. The dissonance inside. To be so heartbroken by Aileen and yet to still want her.

He crumples back into the couch and looks up at the

ceiling. "Why doesn't it ever get easier? This is supposed to get easier."

"Yeah...yeah, it is."

If Kent wants easier, I'm not going to make it harder. "We're in this together, Kent." Harley flashes through my mind. Short, blustering blonde hair, fiery brown eyes, big, gaping smile. I wipe her from the slate of my mind like I've done every moment of every day for the past seven weeks. But now, it's different, because I can't do this to my best friend. I'd rather hurt than cause him the pain of my betrayal. So, I have to let her go. *No more, Grant. No. More.* "We're going to get through this. And...we're going to win."

From the look in his eyes, I don't think he believes me.

And I'm not sure I believe myself either.

I WAKE UP AFTER ANOTHER SLEEPLESS NIGHT IN MY childhood bedroom. Dad has been very keen on keeping all of our rooms just the way that they were when we moved out, which is why there's still a big Australian map on one of my walls with a bunch of thumbtacks pressed into cities and natural landmarks I wanted to go to. I've been meaning to take it down. Australia is a sore spot for me now.

Since I walked in to find my mom on the couch, I haven't had the heart to leave Dad. Lucky for me, Dre is killing it with the show, and I have plenty of vacation days I can throw at this problem. Gina might be pissy with me, but my family is in crisis and I have nothing to lose when I'm now the station's most popular property.

Amy still lives at home and can keep an eye on Dad, but I feel the need to be close to him right now too. It's more of a selfish reason, really. I want to be supportive. But I also just want to be close to him. I'm feeling so vulnerable and small when everything inside me is growing so large. Thoughts about the future, my baby's future, and how my life is going to shift when I become a mom are all so overwhelming.

I just need my daddy sometimes.

There's a quiet knock at my door and I bury my head under the pillow. "Still asleep," I groan, thinking it's Amy trying to get me to go on another one of her morning walks.

"It's Dad."

I push myself up to sitting.

"How are you feeling?"

I swallow. I've been able to attribute my nausea to stress. My mother's untimely arrival certainly hasn't helped in making me feel better. "Okay. Just sleepy."

"I don't blame you."

I can hear him shuffling outside the door. "Do you need something?"

"I–um–I have some coffee cake downstairs. And a coffee if you're feeling like you want to come down and hang out with your old man."

I can't say no to him. Not now. "Sure, give me fifteen."

"Sounds good."

I drag myself out of bed and try to pull myself together. As I pull on an old T-shirt, my hand brushes against the flat of my abdomen. A spark of anticipation runs through me. Won't be flat for too much longer. I cup my belly and look in the mirror. "Be nice to me today, okay?"

I've taken to talking to my little still unnoticeable bump when I'm alone. It's nice to have someone to whisper to in the late-night hours when I can't seem to make sense of my mess of a life. It's also a good distraction from wanting to talk to Grant. It'd be nice to have his deep voice rumbling against my ear, lulling me to sleep. However, I'm staying resolute.

I can't do impulsive things when the ground is so unsteady. Must stay loyal to Dad. On top of that, Dad mentioned that Malcolm is giving Grant a hard time about

Infinium. I'm sure the last thing he wants is to deal with me, his one-time dalliance.

Mother of his child.

I shrug off the stress and make my way downstairs. I find Dad having set out a nice little breakfast for the two of us on the back patio, the centerpiece of which being the coffee cake. I can't get enough of it these days and have had it every morning since I started staying here. "Mmm. Thank you," I say, plopping down in my chair. I'll pretend to sip the coffee and pray Dad doesn't notice I'm not drinking it. Don't want too much caffeine in me.

"Of course. Least I can do to thank you for sticking around and hanging out with...with me," he says with a half-smile.

"No thanks needed. You know that," I say, cutting myself a huge piece of the cake.

"Can't get enough of that stuff, can you?"

I take a huge bite and talk before I've chewed and swallowed. "I don't know. It's addicting."

"Something like that," he says off-handedly.

"You going into the office today?" I ask, sticking my feet up on a neighboring chair.

Dad twists the coffee cup on the table and shakes his head. "I'm meeting up with your mother."

I roll my eyes.

"You could...come with me."

"No. Sorry."

"Harley...I need you to give her a chance."

I stop eating and look at him with ire not meant for him. "Why should I bother? After–"

"Please don't *remind* me."

Things didn't go so well when all the girls came over to see Mom when she arrived the other day. Every question we hurled her way was met with an overly politically correct and saccharine response. Nothing of meaning. No real reason she came other than a "compulsion" she can't seem to describe.

Gillian bubbled with the most anger. "You've missed everything. I don't give a crap about my life; you missed out on five amazing years with *my* daughter. And I'll never forgive you for that."

Dana was miraculously silent the whole time. Of us all, I believe she has been the most betrayed, robbed of her fun college years in order to support the rest of us with everything she had in her.

The conversation ended unceremoniously when we found out Malcolm was also in town. That sealed the deal that her arrival had nothing to do with any of us, but everything to do with *him*.

It's hard to believe that the woman that carried us doesn't want anything to do with us unless it's convenient. I've said as much to my sisters. But not to Dad. He's too raw right now. I don't think he's sleeping either.

"If you are ready to forgive her, then by all means. You do that, Daddy," I say, touching my iced coffee and spinning it around, giving the illusion I'm about to drink it. "But I don't think we are ready for that." The royal we. My sisters. Me. By proxy, my unborn child.

"You don't need to forgive her, but don't you want to..." My dad eyes my hand as I pick up another piece of coffee cake. "Being a mother is hard, Harley."

I try not to let my surprise crop up on my face. It's like he's seeing right through me, seeing what I'm trying to hide. "I know, Dad. But most moms don't walk away, never to be heard from again."

"Not never," he corrects.

"Ten years may as well be never," I rebut.

He blinks and looks away. "You're right. It's a long time. I just don't want you to regret this. Life is...it's shorter than you think. Especially when you have children. They grow so fast and you forget you're growing too." Dad smiles sadly at me.

"Dad, you're fifty. Not on your deathbed," I tease.

"You know that's not my point."

I observe my father for a moment.

When I returned from Australia, I was stunned to realize how old he'd gotten. Deeper wrinkles on his face, gray peppering his dirty blonde hair. It wasn't that he had aged enormously in six years. It's just what happens, I think. Suddenly, you realize your parents are human and they're getting older and one day, in the hopefully very distant future, they'll be gone.

I'm tearing up just thinking about my own little one that is yet to come. He or she will also experience this moment someday too. The moment we realize life is fickle. Temporary. A gift, but not a given.

"You know what's funny?" Dad asks.

I look out at the yard, a morning breeze catching in my hair. "Hm?"

"Your mother loved coffee cake when she was pregnant."

I can't help but do a double-take. "What?"

"Couldn't get enough of it," he goes on with a sentimental smile. "With all of you girls. You don't remember, you were still a baby when Amy came along. But ask Dana, I think she'd...she'd remember."

Dad's eyes are locked on mine. He's trying to say more than he's saying with words. I'm terrified to speak.

"I won't tell anyone, Harley."

Oh my god. He knows. "How did you..."

"I've had five children. I can just tell," he says softly.

I knew he wouldn't be mad when he found out, but for him to know without me telling him. What the hell am I supposed to do with that?

"Same thing happened with Gillian. Except I had to go out of my way to get her the vegan kind and that's—"

I can't help but laugh despite shame pricking at the back of my eyes. "She's so high maintenance."

"So are you, dear."

I blush and look down in my lap.

"Plus, I've been hearing you in the bathroom getting sick and, well, I didn't want to assume anything, but—"

"No, you're right."

Dad swallows, looking at me tenderly.

"I'm pregnant," I say. It's the first time I've said it aloud. And I certainly didn't think the first person I would tell would be my dad.

"Have you been seeing someone or..."

"It's complicated," I say quickly, unable to meet his gaze.

Dad reaches across the table and holds his palm out to me. "I don't need to know anything you aren't ready to tell me."

"Don't tell anyone," I say. "You're the only one who knows."

Dad smiles softly. "I'm honored."

I take his hand and feel like a complete monster for being comforted by his touch. He's sending all his love into me and what have I done in thanks? Slept with his best friend. *Fell* for his best friend. And now I'm having his friend's baby. My father's *grandchild* will belong to Grant in some way, even if Grant never knows it.

I always do things I know won't be good for me. What kind of fucked up person does that?

"I know it's scary," Dad begins again. "I can't imagine how it is from your side of things. But we are all going to be here for you. And...I know if your mother knew, she would be too."

My body tightens. I don't want her near me or my child. Not after the hollow hug and conversations. "It wouldn't be fair to Gillian."

"That's not how life works, Harley."

"It's how it works for me. Right now. That's how it works for me," I say definitively.

Dad purses his lips, then squeezes my hand and nods. "Alright. That's...that's fine. Just think about it, would you?"

"I'll think about it if you can promise me coffee cake every morning I stay here," I say with a sneaking smile.

Dad grins. "I can do that. Anything for you and your..." he leans in and whispers, "you-know-what."

I laugh and, for a moment, let the guilt wash away. Because my dad is along for this adventure with me.

And I hope to keep it that way.

TWENTY

GRANT

When Resa told me that she had arranged for Flick to do a weeklong stint on Harley's radio show, I just about combusted.

For the past two weeks, I have been slaving away over building a case to protect Infinium from Malcolm. I've been going through the back catalogs of old emails and receipts, desperate to find something that will prove that the check he wrote me was *a gift*. His claim might be weak without a contract or anything in writing, but he can make a case against me all he wants as long as he pays the proper lawyers for it.

So, when Resa broke the news of Flick's interview, I admittedly didn't have the best reaction.

"Why the fuck would you do that?!"

"I thought you liked her show!" she said defensively.

Luckily, I was able to couch it in Flick Harrison's antics. "We don't need more visibility on Flick."

"From Harley Solace, I don't think it can hurt. She manages to get people to pour their souls out without sticking their foot in their mouth. I think it's perfect."

I was silent, mind swelling with thoughts of Harley. I never heard back from her. And I'm slightly grateful our will-they-won't-they has come to an end; however unceremonious it was. Life just got too complicated to add another complication to it. Of course, I'm still listening to her show, although one of the weeks, the one right in the wake of Malcolm and Aileen's return, was hosted entirely by her producer Dre.

It was good. But not nearly as good as if Harley had been hosting. And his voice didn't stir my soul quite like Harley's.

Now, she was going to be in my sphere again. And...I just couldn't let well enough alone.

"Let me go with him. Just to prep him and Harley. I don't want him saying something stupid."

"Yeah, or god forbid, hitting on her," Resa said with a snort of laughter.

That statement alone sealed the deal. I was not going to let *Flick Harrison* make a move on my sister and then Harley too. They were both too good for him. And in the case of Harley, well...I couldn't help feeling a little bit possessive. Or a lot, but not like I'm going to act on it.

When Flick and I arrive at the WQXR studio, I've prepped him into oblivion. "No flirting. No crude jokes. No talking about taxes. Got it?" I ask before we walk inside.

Flick smiles slyly. I'm not sure what his eyes are doing behind his dark aviators, but I don't like it. "Yeah, boss. Got it."

"Really, Flick. You're not untouchable. Remember that."

"Trust me, my lawyers remind me of that daily," Flick replies.

I grunt and open the door for him. "We have that in common."

We are not greeted by Harley, but by Dre, who greets me with more praise and acclaim than I deserve. "Mr. Neville, it's such a pleasure to see you again. I've got a spot all set up for you in the booth."

I've decided to accompany Flick on his first day in the studio, evaluate how he does, and then see if I can trust him to make it through the rest of the week without me helicoptering. Of course, if Harley wanted me to return, I wouldn't refuse...

"And Mr. Harrison. I'm such a big fan," Dre says.

"Thank you kindly," Flick drawls.

"Let me show you to the studio. Harley is still prepping some things in her office and–"

"She has an office now, huh?" I ask with a proud smile.

Dre grins. "We've both been upgraded to office-worthy employees. Thanks to your show, Mr. Neville."

I glance around the studio. "Could you point it out to me? I'd like to chat with Harley before we get in the studio. Just about–" I clap my hand on Flick's shoulder. "This piece of work."

Flick laughs. "Is that your pet name for me now?"

"Yes, and you're lucky I don't have you on a literal leash," I murmur.

Dre cackles and I resist telling him I'm not joking. He gestures across the office to a hallway. "Third door on the left. Her name's on it."

"Thanks. You two get settled, I'll be in shortly," I say, already stepping away. My heart pounds as I cross the office and go down the hallway. I don't know what I'm going to say or why I feel compelled to be alone with her. It feels like we've been on opposite sides of this sudden trauma. She's having to deal with Aileen, I'm having to deal with Malcolm. I'm in constant contact with Kent about how he's doing but have no idea how Harley or her sisters are handling it.

It's not my business, I know that. But if I can help, I'd like to.

After all, I'm here, aren't I?

Harley's name *is* on the door, written on a piece of loose-leaf paper in Sharpie. Aw, public radio. I knock softly.

"Yeah!" I hear her shout back. It's not a question. Almost like she's expecting someone.

May as well be me. I open the door slowly and peek inside. "Harley?"

Harley is standing behind a desk on the other side of the room, leaning over a laptop, but her eyes are squarely on me. "What are you doing here?"

"I'm..." I take a step into the room, closing the door almost completely behind me. "I'm here with Flick."

"Oh." Harley looks back to her computer.

Something is wrong. It wouldn't take a psychologist to be able to see that. She looks tired and her usually pretty mop of blonde hair is clipped messily on the back of her head. She's wearing no makeup, not even her signature wings. Still, beautiful as ever. But...

"How have you been?" I ask.

She laughs. It sounds forced. "I think you know the answer to that."

"Yes, I heard about..." Harley leaves her computer to a printer in the corner, waiting for it to start up. "Your mother."

"Yeah..."

I wish she would just turn around and look at me. Give

me a sign that my presence is welcome. But maybe that's the thing. Maybe I'm not welcome.

God, that breaks my heart.

"That must be really tough, Harley. I'm sorry."

She is silent.

I take a couple of steps closer to her. The printer groans to life and she sighs.

"I've been talking with your dad about it, and—"

"Grant, I can't talk to you about my dad. Not now."

Harley is not a particularly tall woman, but she's not tiny either. Right now, she's a shrinking violet, smaller and smaller each second we speak.

Is this my fault? I hope it's not. A few more steps toward her. "You're right. I'm sorry."

Harley takes the documents from the printer and turns, jumping when she realizes how close I've come to her. She freezes, feet planted on the floor.

"I'm not trying to scare you," I say. "Or trying to...you know. I've missed your presence. And I know it's for the best."

"It is."

"Yes, but I've been thinking about you. I care for you. I just want to make sure that you're alright," I say softly, closing in on her inch by inch.

Harley sighs, eyes closing, brow furrowed in pain. "Grant..."

"It's okay, we don't have to talk." I reach out and touch the side of her face. "I'm just here and I'm thinking about you and—"

Aw, fuck it. I'm already here. Might as well go for it. I close the space between us and kiss her softly. Her body is tense and her lips do not bend with mine the way they usually do. And yet, the energy is still there, swirling between us. There's something that just clicks into place with Harley. My mind never goes elsewhere. With Harley, all I'm thinking about is *Harley*.

She slides her hands up my chest and for a second I think she's going to draw me closer. I'm sorely mistaken. Though her fists close for a second pulling me in, the next second she's pushing me away. Our lips part and I immediately utter, "Sorry," so breathlessly I'm not sure she hears it.

"Grant, please don't make me refuse you," Harley says with a pained expression.

I don't know what to say.

"My family is going through so much. My father is..." Harley swallows hard and her jaw is so tense I'm afraid her speaking any more will break it. "We have already gone too far too many times." Finally, fiery brown eyes lift to meet mine. They've never been so cold to me.

"You're right. I'm sorry."

Harley takes a deep breath as if she's about to say something of extreme importance. But she shakes her head. Deciding against it.

"It's alright. Let's just–" She holds up the documents she's just printed. "Let's do the interview and pretend like this didn't happen, alright?"

I feel like I've been stabbed by a thousand arrows. She has every right to refuse me. In fact, I'm so embarrassed I didn't read every signal blaring at me even before I walked into the room. Yet, my heart breaks. Again.

Again and again.

"You have to know it's not because I don't..." Harley gestures between the two of us. "It was never supposed to happen. And we've already made such a mess."

Have we? Does Kent know? Do her sisters know? Are things falling apart even more than I thought possible?

All of these questions, though, I have to keep to myself. I was supposed to keep my distance from her. I've already crossed that boundary.

"You're right. I just want you to know I'm here for you. I care for you and your family." I put my hands in my pockets to keep from touching even her shoulder. "We're going to get through this."

Harley smiles, the tiredness shining through her eyes. "I really hope you're right."

"Me too."

We exchange a smile and then Harley slips past me toward the door. "We should get to the studio."

"Right, yes, of course."

We walk to the studio in silence, me a few steps behind her the whole way. Thank god her body is obscured by a flowy cornflower blue dress. Otherwise, I'd be staring even harder than I already am.

The entire interview goes by in a blur. I keep my head down, listening to Flick and Harley as they banter. Flick's on his best behavior. I have to give him credit for that.

Something is different in Harley's voice. Sure, I could chalk it up to what's happening with her mother. But it's something deeper. Like something has been unlocked inside her.

I wish I knew what it was. Because more than anything—and I mean anything—I wish I could be a part of her life.

However distant that may be.

TWENTY-ONE
HARLEY

"Your palm tree looks like a dick."

I look at Amy beside me in horror. "What?"

She points her paintbrush toward the palm tree on my canvas. "You've placed the coconuts to look like balls."

"Knowing Harley, that was on purpose," Gillian says with a smug smile.

"Guys, please," Dana says softly, focused on her canvas across the table.

"I'm just saying! It's not a palm tree, it's a peen!" Amy announces.

The five of us are having a paint-and-sip party for Amy's twenty-fifth birthday, except the birthday girl is more *chugging* than sipping. I think she's consumed an entire bottle of wine in just under two hours. I haven't been much help there since obviously, I'm not drinking. And my sisters did not take kindly to my refusal.

"New meds," I said when I was met with suspicious looks.

"Oh, what are you on?" Dana asked with genuine curiosity.

I stared at her and blinked. As a grief counselor, she can't prescribe drugs, but she's definitely familiar with them. "Zoloft."

She nodded in understanding. Thank god for that.

"I think I'm finished," I say, sticking my paintbrush into a cup of charcoal gray water.

"No, don't let her get into your head," Gillian says. "You're doing great."

I smile at her gratefully. Maybe I've been less confrontational. Maybe we're all being nicer to each other since Mom showed up. Or maybe Gillian can sense what's going on inside me in some subconscious, maternal way. Regardless, things with her have been easy for the first time in years. We may still rib each other, but it's always followed up with a nicer comment afterward.

Beside me, Amy is going to town on her sunset sky, mixing colors together with reckless abandon. "Okay, now some pink and..." It looks more like a picture in a kid's book than the example painting, which makes sense, obviously.

Across the table, Dana and Kira are near silent as they focus on perfecting their paintings. The class instructor has come over several times to compliment them, leaving Amy flustered and upset.

Then there's Gillian and me. Just...going through the motions. I've been exhausted, now at the two-month mark of my secret-ish pregnancy. On top of all the stress of our mother not backing down from trying to talk to us and Dad trying to *convince* us to talk to her and *Grant* just showing up! Unannounced! Or semi-unannounced.

I'd be lying if I said the idea of Grant accompanying Flick to his interview hadn't crossed my mind.

"You want some fresh air?" Gillian whispers in my ear.

I glance over at her. She's smiling sweetly. The way she does at Stella. Not usually for me.

"The paint fumes are giving me a headache," she adds sheepishly.

"Yeah, yeah. Sounds good."

"Harley and I are going to step out for a minute. Take a breather," Gillian says as we both get up.

"Would you buy us another bottle of wine?" Amy asks eagerly. "We're almost out."

Dana glares at us. "Girls. Don't. She's cut off."

"It's my birthday," Amy whines.

"And if you have any more wine, you're not going to remember it," Dana says simply.

Gillian and I leave our sisters squabbling at their easels, stepping out of the studio and into the cool evening. It's the beginning of September. Getting darker earlier, just slightly.

"You want to walk? It's a nice night," Gillian suggests.

I nod and we start meandering down the sidewalk.

"Thanks," I say to her. "I needed this."

"I could tell," she says, brushing her long blonde hair over her shoulder.

I resist asking how she could tell. I hope it's just sisterly intuition.

"Mom showing up has been hitting you hard, huh?" Gillian asks.

I can feel her eyes on me. I've been avoiding everyone's eyes for weeks now. Ever since I found out I was pregnant. No. Before that. Since Grant came into my life in a really big, really *wrong* way. "I mean, yeah, but it's hit all of us like that, right?"

Gillian sighs. "I guess. Honestly, I've been acting like she never showed up in the first place."

"You still haven't let her meet Stella, huh?"

"Absolutely not," Gillian says. "It'll be a cold day in you-know-where before I do that."

For once, her not swearing is charming to me. Maybe I'm growing a bit softer with motherhood looming in the distance. "You don't think Stella should meet her grandmother?"

Gillian shrugs. "Maybe someday. But...well, I'm not ready for that. Dad thinks I'll regret it, but she's my child. And if I regret it, that's squarely on my shoulders, not his. Besides, there's a lot of life left to live."

"That's funny. He was telling me just a couple of weeks ago how fast life moves once you have kids."

"Oh, it does," Gillian replies. "But that doesn't mean we have to act fast."

"I like that."

She smiles. "For once, you like the way I think."

"Not *for once*."

"Okay, well, maybe this is the first time you've told me," Gillian chuckles.

Man, I haven't been the nicest little sister, have I? So caught up in my own dramas and up my own asshole. "You're a really good mom, Gilly."

"Wow, two compliments in a row! To what do I owe this showering of kindness?"

"I'm trying to be serious."

Gillian slips her arm through mine as we walk. "I know, I know. Sorry. Thank you, that means a lot. Like *a lot* a lot."

"How do you do it? Must be hard being a single mom."

"I get *a lot* of help," she says pointedly.

"Not just that, but emotionally. It must be weird."

Gillian's face screws together tight. "I guess it can be.

You'd be surprised, though. A lot of women end up in my position."

Yeah. Me. I almost tell her right then and there but decide against it. That would be a big burden for her to bear in front of all our sisters.

"I don't have regrets if that's what you're wondering."

"I know you don't. You made a choice. I've always respected it." I was in Australia when I found out Gillian was pregnant. She had tasked Dana with telling me. I've always nursed that as a minor heartbreak, that Gillian didn't tell me herself. At the time, I was so steeped in my own bull-shit, I barely paid mind to it. Maybe that broke Gillian's heart as well. "And Stella is just the best."

Gillian smiles. "She really is." Then she looks over at me, eyebrow raised. "Why are you bringing this up?"

"Uhm. I don't know."

"Uh-huh."

"I don't!"

"I just said 'uh-huh'!"

We both laugh. The laughter peters out into a comfort-able silence. I don't remember the last time Gillian and I were alone this long. I think we've both avoided it.

"Thanks for saying that, Harley. I've always thought you see me as some sort of fuck-up."

"You?! A fuck-up? Gillian, that's insane!"

She nervously laughs. "I don't know. Maybe."

"You own a business, you're a mom, and you are really strong in your beliefs, even if I think bacon is too good to give up."

"Don't forget cheese."

"God, you vegans."

Gillian chuckles. "I don't know, Harley. I've sort of

come by everything in life by accident. You've always had so much purpose and drive. I guess I'm a little jealous."

If only she knew just how unplanned my life is. Then she'd be singing a different tune. "Gillian, everything in life is accidental. Literally, every single thing."

"I guess you're right."

I can feel her beating herself up inside. She doesn't fully believe me. Not yet. Soon, she'll realize just how similar we are. Once I get the courage to let her know. "What's your favorite part about being a mom?"

Gillian gasps. "Oh. That's a hard question."

"Take your time."

We walk a long while in silence, rounding the block in the process.

"There are lots of things. But I think it's when she comes to me with her big problems. And you know, a five-year-old's big problems aren't that big in the scheme of things, but to her, they are." Gillian looks off into the distance. I focus on the beauty mark along her jaw. When I was a kid, I'd press it and say, "Polka dot!" and she'd always get mad. I think it's beautiful now. "Knowing that she will come to me for comfort. That I can give her what she needs and grow with her. It's special."

Without realizing it, there are tears in my eyes. "That's beautiful, Gilly."

"You want to know what's even better than that?"

"What?"

Gillian stops. Her face is hardened. Determined. "Knowing I won't ever do to her what our mom did to us. Ever."

I feel my heart sink. It hadn't even crossed my mind, the thought of doing what our mom did. But what if that's somehow ingrained in us? "How can you be sure?"

Her eyes dart to me. "Because I will never care about myself more than Stella. Ever."

My baby is not yet big enough to move around, but there is a phantom motion in my body, my baby is already so real to me that I can feel them. I already feel what Gillian feels.

"Gilly?"

"What, Harl?"

"Would you come on my podcast?"

Gillian leaps away from me, hands to her face. "Seriously?"

I laugh. I've never had my sisters on the show for fear of familiarity bungling the integrity of the interview. I think it's time I start. "Sure. You can bring Lola too if you want."

"Harley!" she squeals and throws her arms around me, squeezing me so tight I actually start to worry for my tiny baby. "You have no idea how much that would mean to me!"

I hug her back, and for a moment, the drama melts away. I push my face into my sister's hair, smell the lavender essential oil she dabs behind her ears, and I feel small again.

Gosh, things felt so much easier when I was small.

Now, I'm a grown woman who was abandoned by her mother, brokenhearted in Australia, and having a baby all by herself.

It's impossible for the baby to cross my mind without Grant crossing it too. He's given me this joy. And I wish I could share that joy with him. He'd make an amazing father. I really believe that. I know it can never be. Especially not now.

Even though I set the boundary with him at the studio only a few days ago...I wish he'd cross it just one more time.

I might just give in to him.

TWENTY-TWO
GRANT

MALCOLM JENKINS. IN THE FLESH. HE LOOKS LIKE *THE Picture of Dorian Grey*. Last I saw him, he made me jealous with his good looks. Now, we're ten years older. And he looks it.

When he walks into the conference room, I'm stunned to see that my old friend (ex-friend) doesn't look at all like he once did. Sure, we've both gotten older, but I like to think I don't look a day over thirty-nine, thank you very much.

Not only has he gained a bit of weight around the middle, but his jowls are starting to hang down. I believe he's gotten Botox from how little his forehead moves. Or maybe he just genuinely has no emotions in that big head of his.

More noticeable than anything is how ill-fitting his suit is.

The old Malcolm Jenkins would never be caught dead in a suit even slightly tight on him. It's obvious, however, from how he moves his arms and legs, that the suit is from a time long gone.

Which begs the question: does he not have money for a

new suit? Could this be why he's coming for me? That he's run out of money?

I can't imagine all of his investments have fallen through or that he could have possibly burned through all the money he's made over the years. Maybe Aileen could, though.

I stand up from the spot between my lawyers. *Keep it cordial, Grant.* "Malcolm," I greet him, taking a step toward him and holding out my hand. "Good to see you."

I've never noticed how insidious he looks when he smiles. He takes my hand. His palm is clammy. "Old friend. You look well."

Wish I could say the same.

"My money looks good on you."

Damn. I guess he's still the same underhanded person who betrayed Kent. Never missing a chance to bring someone to where he feels he is above them. Well, I'm glad I'm stronger than that. Above that.

I drop my hand from his "Well, seems like you'd like to just jump right in?"

"No need to beat around the bush, right?" Malcolm says with a smile. A few more wrinkles in his cheeks than there used to be.

We take a seat with our respective lawyers across a large conference table from one another. I've opted to keep this out of court...for now. But I'm not budging even a little bit. My lawyers are prepared for this. I'm sure Malcolm's are too. If there's any way at all we can keep it from going into the courts and on the public record, I'm all for it.

As we sit across the table, eyeing each other, I can't believe how sour things have gone. Back in the day, Malcolm, Kent, and I were a triumvirate. Even though I had Victoria to care for and couldn't live at the fraternity house, we were always together. I know Victoria even had a childish crush on Malcolm when she was little.

Unlike me, she has never crossed the line with my friends. And even if she did, a friend dating my sister would sit differently than a friend dating a daughter. I may not have one, but just being on the other side of it doesn't make it hard to recognize the gravity of the line I've crossed.

No thinking about Harley. Business only. My constant mantra these days.

Malcolm leans back in his chair and starts to bounce. "Swanky place you've got here."

"We keep it nice."

"I bet you do," he says and then leans forward, clasping his palms on the table. "So, have you come to your senses?"

I glance at one of my lawyers, Francis, a young attorney with a swoop of black hair, frameless glasses that sometimes look invisible on his face. He makes a note on his legal pad but doesn't say anything. "My senses? What might those be?"

Malcolm laughs. "I take that as a no."

"Let's be real, Malcolm. Neither of us wants to do this in court, right?"

He rolls his eyes smarmily. "Maybe *you* don't want to do it in court. I, on the other hand, don't feel encumbered by... sentimentality. As it were."

"I'm not encumbered by it either."

"Oooh...Grant, I'm not so sure about that," Malcolm replies with condescension dripping off every word. "I know you and Kent must have had plenty of good times without me over the years. You're on your high horse about being a good friend, holding onto that legacy. Right?"

"That's a very strange way of putting all of that."

Malcolm crosses his arms over his chest. I see the seams on his shoulders strain. "How would you tell it, then?"

I frown. "You really want me to go there?"

"I know you've been waiting to chew me out for ten years. May as well have a go."

He's asking for me to be the asshole. That means I'll be giving him some sort of satisfaction. And that's the last thing I want to do. "I don't think we're going to get anywhere with this. Behind closed doors without a judge present." I turn to Malcolm's lawyers, two men that almost look like identical twins with their balding nests of hair and thin lips. "I'm sorry to have wasted your time, gentlemen. I look forward to the opportunity to work this all out in a more appropriate setting."

Malcolm scowls. "Really, Grant? We just got started."

"And now it's over," I say, getting to my feet and buttoning my suit jacket. "Now, I'll have to ask you to–"

Malcolm slams his fist down on the table. "I'm not going anywhere. This is my company too, Grant."

"Like hell it is," I snap. Then, without another word, I leave the conference room. Fuck being nice. Fuck decorum. If he wants a fight, he'll get it. I guarantee it.

ANOTHER DAY IN HOLLYWOOD, another award ceremony. This time, it's a simple gala being held in honor of Tilly Quarterman, a legend of stage and cinema. Tilly's nearing a century old, yet she still has the energy and gumption to get up on stage and give us all nearly fifteen minutes of comedic material. It's brilliant and an honor to be in the same room as the legend.

I've come alone this time. Victoria is in New York

preparing for Fashion Week. And I haven't had a legit date to one of these things in years. Besides, I want to see who I need to see and get out of there as fast as possible.

After the acceptance speech comes the general milling about that we do. It's a rather stodgy event, the average age definitely higher than fifty.

Which is how I spot Harley without even batting an eye.

As usual, she takes my breath away. Donning a loose boho gown with her hair clipped on the back of her head, she looks like she's just stepped out of Woodstock. She's standing at the bar, pointing at a bottle of club soda. The bartender smiles and nods. And as she waits, I watch her.

Still she looks so tired. Concerned. Malcolm might be a thorn in my side, but I can't imagine how it's been for her to deal with Aileen.

Harley must feel me looking at her. She turns her head, her brown eyes immediately finding mine, almost locking into place. *Click.*

I don't move a muscle. She told me to stay away and that's what I'll do. Ignore every impulse to run over to her and see how she's doing. I force a smile.

Harley sadly smiles back.

This is what we deserve for betraying Kent. Doomed to an eternity of wondering what could have happened between us. I've done enough daydreaming for a lifetime. I want to know what it's like for Harley to be mine and vice versa.

Not in this world. Perhaps another.

We haven't even spoken a word and yet my heart breaks.

The bartender returns with a small bottle of club soda and Harley takes it, cracking it open and swigging it as she turns away, darting through a crowd of people toward the exit.

As she leaves, my body is compelled to follow despite my mind telling me not to. "Harley..." I say softly, not loud enough for anyone to hear me. "Excuse me," I mutter as I wade through the groups of guests. "Harley!" I call out louder.

She slips through the front door and runs smack into someone else I recognize.

Aileen.

TWENTY-THREE
HARLEY

"Mom, what the hell are you doing here?" I cry out, dropping the club soda I desperately needed to settle my stomach. The plastic bottle hits the ground, liquid fizzing on the pavement.

My mother's hands lock around my upper arms as she pulls me close. "I need to talk to you."

"How did you find me?" I ask, starting to struggle in her grip.

"Your father mentioned you'd be here."

I can't believe he's still entertaining her. Trying to get us girls to give her a chance when it's become more than apparent she's here for one reason and it has nothing to do with us. "Let go of me," I grunt, trying to pull away.

But my mother's grip is strong. Her fingers dig into my arms. "Come with me. I have a car. We can talk."

"There's nothing to talk about!" I yelp. "Now let *go!*"

As the two of us struggle, a flash of light appears in the corner of my eye. Jesus Christ, someone's recording this. How embarrassing. The last thing I need is for something like this to end up on the internet.

"I'm your mother, Harley!"

"You don't–" I wriggle. "Act like it!"

"I've apologized! What more could you–"

"Let *go of me!*" I shout at the top of my lungs, finally gathering the last bit of strength I can muster to push her away from me. I stumble back and try to catch my breath. But something is wrong. I'm lightheaded and the lights of Hollywood are spinning in my eyes. "Fuck."

"Harley..."

I feel my mother's hand on my shoulder.

"Don't *touch* me."

"Something's wrong, you're–"

She's right. Something *is* wrong. That's the last thing I hear before my vision blurs and my knees give out.

The next thing I know, I'm bobbing in someone's arms. The left side of my body is sore and I think I hit my head. I open my eyes, but they won't focus no matter where I look.

"What's...what happe—"

"Just rest. It's going to be okay."

I know that voice. I know the feeling of these arms. But I can't place it, I'm too...tired, too lost, too disoriented to even know which way is up. I close my eyes again, praying this nightmare will be over when I wake up.

"Oh, her eyelashes are fluttering."

"You're seeing things."

"I'm not!"

I blink my eyes open to a blurry face leaning over me.

"She's awake!" The voice belongs to Amy. "I told you her eyelashes–"

"Yeah, yeah, whatever." There's Gillian.

"Okay, girls, just relax, don't crowd her, alright?" I hear Dad interrupt. He leans over me. My eyes start to focus a bit more and his features sharpen. "Harley? Are you okay? Can you hear me?"

"Yeah..." My voice comes out all muted and strange. I reach up to my mouth. My hand hits a plastic oxygen mask.

Dad touches my wrist softly. "Now, let's just leave this on until–"

"I want it off," I say. The warm air is making me feel strangled. I yank the mask down and take a deep breath of... stale hospital air. Maybe I should have left it on. "What happened?"

Dad glances around the room at my sisters and sits on the bed next to me. "You had a little accident, sweetheart. You fainted. But everything is okay and–"

"And your baby is okay too!" Amy squeaks and then slaps her hand over her mouth.

Dad sighs. "*Amy...*"

"How do you know about–" I sit up too quickly and feel the blood rush to my head.

"Whoa, whoa, whoa, easy." Dad gestures to Dana. "Help me with the pillows, would you?"

Dana and Dad fluff the limp hospital pillows behind me. "Thanks," I mutter before eyeing Amy again.

She's standing almost like a child who has gotten caught sneaking a cookie from the cookie jar.

"Well?"

"I mean, it's kind of Dad's fault."

"*Amy,*" Dad scolds.

"Dad!" I scold too.

"I..." Dad rubs his hands over his eyes. "I had to tell the doctors that it was something to look out for since I suspected that you might be. I'm sorry, Harley, I was just worried."

I look up at my dad. The worry is clear in every nook and cranny. The thin line of his mouth, his furrowed brow, the sad corners of his eyes. This man has been put through way too much lately and I'm just making it worse. I'm sure he rushed over here as soon as he heard. But how did he hear? That's still a mystery.

Gillian puts her hand on my shoulder, wearing an endearing smile. "You knew, didn't you?"

I feel a smile creep up on my lips and nod. "Yeah, yeah I did."

She wraps her arms around me. "Congratulations."

I bury my face in her shoulder. "Thanks, Gilly."

"You and I have a lot to talk about," she says and then adds with a dry laugh, "*A lot* a lot."

"Yes, we do. I need all your expertise." When she draws away and I get a good look at everyone, I can see the joy on their faces. Kira's clearly been crying while Dana rubs her back and Amy is obviously bouncing with excitement.

"Who is the dad, Harley?" Amy asks with a grin.

"Let's not overwhelm her too much, alright?" Dana says, holding up her hand. "She'll tell us when she's ready."

I mouth, "Thank you," to her and she nods simply. It doesn't take a rocket scientist to connect the dots. She knows that this is going to be a big bomb dropped on the family.

If I ever decide to tell them.

"How did I get here?" I ask.

"Your..." Dad clears his throat. "Your mother called to tell us that she was with you when it happened."

I glance around the room. "Where is she?"

"I don't think she came with, sweetheart. She said Grant offered to bring you here."

My heart flutters. Grant brought me here? No wonder I knew the voice and the arms. He was taking care of me. Of our baby...and he didn't even know it.

Then Dad looks away. "She asked me to give her a call when you woke up."

I laugh, though my heart breaks. "I don't know how she manages to keep getting worse, and yet..."

"I'm sorry, honey," Dad murmurs and wraps his arm around my shoulder. "I shouldn't have told her you were there; it was my mistake. I just..." His eyes are welling with tears. I've seen my dad cry more than most. It breaks my heart every time. "Knowing that you girls are growing up and having your own babies without her there. Just hurts me so much."

I cup my dad's cheek. Fuck my mom. I don't know if she ever even wanted to be one. And that's its own kind of heartache. But I know this man wanted me and each of my sisters beyond compare. "The people who matter are here."

A few tears stream down his face. "Yeah..."

"None of us have missed out on a drop of love with you around, Dad. I promise." I wrap my arms around him. Dad starts to cry. I wave to my sisters. "Come on, get in here."

The Solace sisters all gather around our dad, hugging the ever-living daylights out of him.

These are the people who matter. The ones I would do anything for.

Even denying myself the father of my baby. If that can protect my dad from any more hurt, so be it.

I've got everything I need right here.

TWENTY-FOUR
GRANT

Yellow roses are supposed to be a flower of friendship. At least that's what Google says. So that's what I've brought with me, a big bouquet of yellow roses to make it abundantly clear to Harley and the Solace family that this is just a visit of *friendship*.

Nothing more.

I walk up to the Solace front door. A fateful image. The last time I was here was the Fourth of July party. Before everything...happened. This feels like déjà vu.

I ring the doorbell and wait, nervously tapping my foot. I was hoping that Harley might be at her home, but when I texted Kent to check in on her, he told me she was staying with him for the next few days. *Dehydrated. I keep telling that girl to drink water!* was the text he sent.

Perhaps that's why she ordered the club soda at the event last night.

Apart from Kent, where there is one Solace girl, there are surely several more to follow. That's evident from all the vehicles in the driveway, the most eye-catching of which being Harley's Harley.

When the door swings open, I'm face to face with Kent. He's beaming at me. There's appreciation in his eyes. "There he is! The hero!"

I'm sure he wouldn't be calling me a hero if he knew the other things I'd done for his daughter. *To* her. *With* her.

"Oh, I'm not a–" Kent pulls me into a bear hug, knocking the wind out of me. The flowers narrowly escape his embrace.

"No, you are," he says, patting my back. "Thank goodness you were there." Kent pulls back, eyes glimmering. "You're a true friend, Grant."

I feel like I'm being pranked. Are there hidden cameras? Did Harley tell him and now he's waiting for me to admit everything in some sort of "gotcha" moment?

"Could I see her? I brought some flowers?"

"Of course," Kent says and ushers me inside. "She's in her room. Girls! Say hi to Grant!"

Three of the other four Solace girls poke their heads out of the kitchen like a scene out of *The Brady Bunch*. "Hi Grant!" they say in unison.

"Gosh, you girls are like a choir of angels singing in harmony," I say.

"Too bad none of them can carry a tune to save their lives," Kent says. The girls all balk and protest. Kent only laughs. "I'm just *kidding*. Come on, I'll show you her room."

Up the stairs, into the depths of the Solace house, I go. I can almost feel Harley's energy through the walls. Each and every step bringing me closer to her.

"Here we are," Kent announces when we reach the door at the end of the hallway. On it is an old piece of paper with the words "Keep Out" written in Sharpie. "You'll forgive her manners," Kent jokes, pointing to the sign.

I can't manage a laugh, much more focused on calming my nerves than the conversation.

Kent knocks. "Harley? I've got a visitor here for you. He brought flowers."

"Come in."

Her voice sounds so meek and tired. Between the stress of Aileen's return and the dehydration, she must be laid out pretty low.

Kent opens the door and gestures for me to go through first. The second I step into her room, I'm transported back to middle school. Of course, my room never looked like that of a teen girl's. But that energy is there. Childlike and incohesive. It's charming and also...makes me feel even more guilty than I already was.

"Grant. Hi," Harley says, pushing herself up out of the bed.

God, she looks great. It goes without saying at this point. She's wearing a huge Iron Maiden T-shirt that she's practically swimming in, curled up with her laptop. A work-from-home sort of day. I'd love to have that sort of day with her. Lazy. In bed. I would wait on her hand and foot. "Um. Hi."

"Grant wanted to check that you were doing alright," Kent says, saving me from my inability to form coherent thoughts.

"And he brought flowers," Harley remarks with a smile.

Shit, the flowers. "Um, yes. Yeah. I did." I walk closer to her bed, which feels practically illegal, and hand the flowers over to her.

"Yellow...they're beautiful." Harley takes a deep inhale. "Mm. They smell wonderful. Thank you."

I try not to audibly gulp.

"Daddy, could you put these in some water?" Harley asks.

"Of course, sweetie." Kent takes the flowers and gives her a kiss on the forehead. I have to look away. Feels wrong for me to even be here after everything that's happened.

Playing with fire, Neville...

"I'll give you two a moment alone. I'm sure Harley has some thanking to do," Kent says as he flits out the door. It hangs open, which is for the best. That'll keep me from doing anything too stupid.

"Really, Grant, thank you for the flowers," Harley breaks the silence in a gentle voice.

"Of course, it's the least I can do."

She laughs, "I mean, you brought me to the hospital. I feel like I owe *you* at this point."

I shake my head. "Are you kidding? That's...I'm sorry I couldn't do more."

"Well, you would have needed a medical degree for that," Harley replies with dry humor.

I try to laugh, but I can't. "Seeing you there like that..."

"Grant—"

"No, I need you to know. Just let me say it and then I'll shut up. I promise."

Harley closes her mouth and looks down into her lap.

"Seeing you on the ground like that and—" My eyes are starting to well up. "You know, I know things between us are fucked up but that...that would have just killed me, I think." I've tried to block the image from my memory. The thought of what could have happened to her if I wasn't there...well, maybe Aileen would have been forced to step up then. I'm safer than Aileen, though. I care about who Harley is *now*, not about the child she once was. If Aileen even cares about that.

"Grant, come here." Harley extends her hand toward me. "Come sit."

How can I resist her when she's literally asking for me to be close? The thing I've wanted all this time.

I take her hand and immediately feel the fire of her touch. I can't resist it. Like running from a forest fire. Nearly impossible. I sit on the bed beside her and cup both my hands around hers. "Harley..."

"Thank you for taking care of me," she murmurs.

"Of course."

"You didn't have to."

"I did. Of course, I did," I reply.

"You could have walked away."

I furrow my brow. "Why would I have–"

"Left all this alone."

"I couldn't just leave you there."

Her lower lip trembles. "I don't deserve it."

"What the hell are you talking about?" I wrap my hand around the side of her face. "How can you say that?"

Harley's brown eyes meet mine. Something unsaid lies behind them. I won't pry. I know her constitution right now is weak. But I can't help but wonder if she's keeping in the same thing I am. That my heart, despite every attempt to deny it, is entirely dedicated to her.

"What's going on?"

Kent. I turn to look in horror. He's standing in the doorway with a crystal vase full of the yellow roses. So much for friendship, I guess.

"Daddy, it's not–" Harley pushes me away. "We were just talking about what happened and..."

She can try and talk her way out of it all she wants, but the look on Kent's face is enough to let me know he understands exactly what's going on. He looks at me, jaw lolling open in shock. This is what I was afraid of. That look of betrayal.

I get up and start to approach Kent. "Why don't you and I go talk about this privately and let Harley rest while–"

"Okay!" Dana's voice comes from down the hall, footsteps drawing closer.

Shit. Everything in the Solace house ends up a family affair. I should have known way better.

"I ended up getting you minestrone because the chicken noodle was so high in sodium," Dana announces, forcing herself into the doorway next to Kent. "Can't imagine that's too good for the baby..."

"Baby?" I echo in confusion.

Dana finally sees me. Her face goes completely pale. "Grant. Hi."

"What...baby?" I ask. The silence in the room answers my question. I look from Dana's ghostly face to Kent whose shock is morphing into anger by the second, and then to Harley who...won't even look at me.

Oh my god. Harley is pregnant. And by the silence in the room, I think it's pretty clear who is the father.

Me.

My head is spinning. "I should go," I say meekly, taking a few steps to the door.

Dana steps out of the way to let me through, but as I pass Kent, he grabs me by the arm, wrenching my eyes into his. I've never been on the receiving end of Kent Solace's ire, at least not like this. His whole face is tense like a volcano waiting to blow, steam practically pouring from his ears.

"Daddy, please, don't," Harley whimpers from the bed. The tears are starting to spill from her eyes. "Please let me explain before you get mad. Let him go."

The anger drops from his face at the sound of his

daughter begging. "Of course, Harley. I'll..." He lets go of me and turns away from me. "I'll deal with him later."

Harley looks at me. *Go*, her eyes say.

I leave without another word, relinquishing any semblance of control I thought I had. Kent now knows. And Harley's pregnant. And though I have a well of questions as deep as the sea, I know that I'm no longer welcome at the Solace house.

It was only a matter of time before everything came to light. Grant and me. Grant's baby. I thought I'd have control over how the information was presented, be able to modulate the shock and high-octane emotions.

Instead, it all blew up in my face all at once. If this weren't my life, I think I'd laugh.

However, it is my life. Not only is everything dramatic, but I'm also having to deal with it while riding out the symptoms of pregnancy. The mood swings are in *full* effect. I've been crying off and on since Dad walked in and found Grant in me in a relatively tame position, yet a position, nonetheless.

He didn't take it well. I think if I hadn't been there, he would have had a royal rumble with Grant right here in the house. I can only remember one other time my dad was angry enough to be violent...when his other so-called best friend betrayed him.

Now, I've isolated my dad, given him no one to trust. I feel like a monster.

I've talked Dad down as best as I could with my sisters

at my side, uneaten soup having gone cold on the night-stand. Gillian, Amy, and Kira came up after seeing Grant leave in a hurry and crowded in the doorway. Thought I might as well get the story out in one go.

Dana has been at my side this whole time. She's been supportive in her silence, holding my hand and rubbing my back as I try to explain to my dad what he's just seen. How sorry I am. I try to take the brunt of the blame, saying that I was the one who seduced him, that Grant's not to blame.

I don't think my dad is buying it or even cares, though. His expression is serious and dower and he's barely uttering more than "mhm" and "uh-huh".

"So, that's what happened. And I'm really sorry, Daddy. I didn't mean for all this to..." I trail off. I don't know if I can manage an apology for getting pregnant. Not when I now feel it's the next right step in my journey.

Dad licks his lower lip and takes a deep breath. "I can't say I'm not disappointed."

"Daddy," Gillian scolds. "That's not fair."

"It's okay, Gillian." I look down into my lap. "I understand."

His face is as hard as stone. "Grant knew much better than to cross the line like he did. You're just a kid."

"I'm not a kid," I say vehemently. "I'm *your* kid. There's a difference."

Dana squeezes my shoulder, and I can feel the energy of the rest of my sisters bolstering me. There are very few things any of us could do to make us lose support from the rest of us. I'm very grateful for that.

"I knew what I was doing. I was there and I made a choice. It just got a little out of control."

Dad's eyebrows jump. "You're pregnant, Harley. That's more than a little out of control."

My face is raw from tears, yet more fall. "I'm sorry."

"Dad, give her a break. She's overstimulated," Dana murmurs.

Dad takes a moment before getting up from the bed. "I need some time to think."

I curl my legs up and bury my face in my knees to sob. I can't watch him go, not after I watched Grant leave so bewildered by the news of my pregnancy. It's already been too much.

Dana wraps her arms around me. "It's going to be okay, Harley."

"No, it's not."

I feel Amy leap onto the bed next to me and join the hug. "Yes, it is."

Then Gillian. "We promise."

"He'll never forgive me," I sob.

The last Solace sister joins the group hug, Kira with her limitless simplicity of wisdom. "Of course he will, you're his daughter."

I shake my head. "He has four more. He can lose one."

"Now you're just being mean to yourself," Dana admonishes, squeezing my shoulder.

Feeling all my sisters crowded around me settles my pounding heart. For the first time since Grant left, my tears feel fully abated. "Grant..." I croak. So many thoughts I can't express. His name the only thing I can find.

"I can't say I saw that coming," Amy remarks.

"You must think I'm disgusting," I say.

"As long as you wanted to do it, I don't think we have room to judge," Gillian says.

I raise my gaze to Gillian. She's being so nice to me. Our newfound identity as mothers has bridged the gap more than I could have anticipated. And I couldn't be more grateful.

"Besides, from an objective standpoint," Kira says, pushing up her glasses. "Grant is a specimen."

We all look at her and burst into laughter. Kira is so spare in sharing her feelings about men that it takes us all by surprise.

"Now, this is a picture-perfect moment."

My sisters and I go silent at the sound of my mom's voice. As if I haven't been taken off-guard enough today, here she is in the door to my room, perfectly dressed and manicured, looking more like a Stepford wife than a mother.

"What are *you* doing here?" Dana asks, tightening her arm around me.

"I came by to check on Harley. But what a pleasant surprise to see all my girls in one place," she says, her veneers glowing white.

It is remarkable when all of us Solace girls are silent. Our mother is probably about the only thing that can take the words out of our mouths.

She floats into the room and sits at the foot of the bed. "How are you feeling, Harley?"

"Better, thanks," I sniff.

Mom smiles sweetly. I used to long for this. My mother at the end of my bed, here to comfort me. Now it sours my stomach. "You gave us all quite a fright last night."

"Is that why you let Grant take her to the hospital?" Dana questions.

"Dana, it's okay," I whisper.

My eldest sister sits up straight, daggers in her eyes. "No. It's not."

"Dana, dear, I didn't think Harley would want me to

help her. You've all made it very clear that I'm not welcomed here, so–"

"And yet, here you are. Besides, whose fault is that?" Dana shoots back. "You waltz back into our lives after *ten years* and expect to be welcomed? What kind of mother does that?"

Mom lifts her chin. "I've made mistakes. I'm not proud of everything I've done. But I'd like to atone for–"

"For nothing." Dana is going in for the kill. "You came here with Malcolm because you want *money*. You're just an accessory to this lawsuit he has with Infinium and–"

"You weren't supposed to know about that."

"Why? So you can pretend that you give a shit about any of us?" Dana's shouting now. I never hear her yell. She's got the sweetest lilt of us all, perfect to care for the emotions of others. But inside her is anger that has been brewing for ten whole years. "I'd like you to leave. You don't have a place here."

Mom's eyes widen. "Dana, I'm your mother. You can't–"

"Yes, you are my mother. Who walked away from me when I was nineteen, the oldest of five girls. Who do you think did everything you were supposed to while they were growing up, huh?" Dana growls like a mother lion protecting her cubs. "*Me*. I did. Who mothered *me* in all of this?"

The other four of us are quiet. We've done our best to take care of each other, but Dana has taken on the brunt of mothering.

"Your father–"

"Did everything he could for us when you left," Dana says sharply. "But he could never be our *mother*."

There is a standoff. The silence is deep and profound.

"I'll walk you out," Dana says, getting to her feet.

"Dana!" Mom gasps.

"This is our house. Not yours. And you are not welcome here. Now, you can leave of your own accord. Or I'll make you."

I resist cheering for Dana. It would undercut the moment. But *hell fucking yeah.*

Mom stands to her feet and straightens out her skirt. "Fine." She looks at the rest of us, almost like she'll say something, but decides against it, her lips dropping with shame.

Good.

Dana ushers Mom through the door and follows her down the stairs.

The four of us share a sigh. "Wow. We owe Dana like, big time," Amy says.

"You can say that again," Kira adds.

We collapse back on my bed, staring up at the ceiling. "What a fucking summer, huh?" I say.

"Emphasis on the 'fucking'," Amy echoes.

We giggle, even Gillian.

Our reverie is interrupted by Dana's footsteps fast on the stairs. "Guys! Dad is–" She catches herself in the doorframe. "Dad's car is gone."

I sit up immediately. "Oh no."

"You think he went to see Grant?"

"I know he did," I say and start to get out of bed.

Gillian grabs my shirt. "Harley, you need rest. Don't get involved, it's not–"

I wave her off and start to stumble around the room looking for my keys. "I have to. I'm the one who made this mess. I can't let it get any worse. Grant is..." I sigh. "Grant is the only friend Dad has. I can't be responsible for ruining their friendship."

"I don't think you're going to stop her, Gillian," Kira mutters.

"Well, you're not riding on your scooter," Gillian says, crossing her arms over her chest.

I glower. "It's a motorcycle."

"I'll drive her," Dana announces.

I smile at Dana, though my heart breaks. She was born into this role. The eldest. The maternal one. And she'll never be able to step away from it, no matter how she tries. "Thanks, D."

Dana jerks her head into the hall. "Come on. I don't want to find them in a half Nelson."

We rush out of the house to Dana's car. The second my seatbelt clicks, I notice how hard my heart is pounding and the adrenaline rushing through my veins. I'm ready to fight for my life and what I want.

Mom might have been a crappy mother. But she did teach me a lesson about not denying ourselves the things that we want. She ended up breaking things in the process. I'm not going to make *that* mistake.

For once, I'm going to be my mother's daughter. I'm not denying myself what I want any longer. However, unlike her, I'm going to *build* something. Something beautiful.

TWENTY-SIX

GRANT

"THANK GOD YOU'RE HERE," I SAY WHEN I FIND Victoria in my living room.

"What's going on? What's the emergency?" she asks, eyes wide with worry.

I texted her when I left the Solace house for her to meet me here. I needed someone to talk to. The only person who understands all my fears. "Okay, I'm just going to come out with it and I need you to save your questions for later."

"Oh, Jesus, this sounds bad already."

"Tor!"

"I'm just saying!" Victoria looks around. "God, let me sit before you drop any bombs on me." She perches on a leather armchair. "Alright, go ahead."

I take a breath. *Out with it.* "I've been falling for Harley Solace and she might be pregnant with my baby."

Victoria grabs at her chest like she's just been shot. "What?"

"Fourth of July, the two of us ended up sort of–"

"You fucked Kent's kid?!"

I wince. "Don't say it like that."

"I'm sorry, I just didn't expect this of all things to be–"

"Let me just tell the story and then you can rip me a new one, alright?"

Victoria huffs. "Fine."

I explain the events as best I can to her without making her cringe. How we kept falling together, unable to resist, how I've never felt this way about someone and knew how it would break Kent's heart if he found out, and how shit hit the fan less than two hours ago.

"And she's pregnant but you don't know if it's yours?" Victoria asks with a raised eyebrow.

"So, this is what I've just found out," I explain. "Right after Kent walked in on us, Dana walked in and was like, 'I got this soup for the baby' and, well, I just assumed it was mine, but I guess–"

"I think it's a safe assumption."

"Okay, so then, Harley Solace is pregnant with my baby." The weight of what I've just said punches me in the gut. I collapse into the couch. "Holy shit."

The room is silent.

"Congratulations, brother."

"Is it congratulations?"

Victoria smiles. "Yeah, I think so."

I rub my hands over my face. "Fuck."

"Grant, isn't this what you've wanted?"

I sigh. "Victoria, you know as well as I do–"

"Don't bring Mom and Dad into this."

Our blue eyes meet. Silence.

"They aren't a part of this."

I shake my head. "Of course they are. They're the whole reason we're here."

"And they've been gone for thirty years."

Thirty years. Wow. I hadn't realized how much time had gone by. "I'm not good for anyone, Victoria."

"That's a bullshit self-preservation tactic and you know it," Victoria replies. "I'm sick of watching you talk yourself out of what you want because you're scared you're going to fuck up. Grant, you're not them."

"We don't know that."

Victoria throws her hands up in the air. "I mean, maybe I don't *know*, but I have a pretty good inkling that you're not going to repeat their mistakes."

I appreciate her vote of confidence even if I don't believe it. "Well, I don't even know if Harley would want me involved or how she feels or–"

"Then you should just tell her."

Well, that sounds scary as hell.

"Kent knows now, right."

"Yeah, and that's going to be a whole other thing to deal with entirely."

"Okay, well, forget about him. He knows now, so there's no reason to hold back how you feel." Victoria looks me dead in the eye. "How do you feel, Grant?"

The entire car ride home, my whole body felt like it was twisting in on itself with confusion, unsure if I'd heard correctly or if it was even me who was responsible.

Now, I think it's fair to assume that I'm a part of this.

I've always feared love and fatherhood after seeing how horrible things turned out with my parents. In fact, I've actively avoided any possibility of love. For the first time, with Harley, I've been eager to run into the fire. That's got to mean something. "I think I want a chance with her. Because I..."

Victoria speaks for me. "You love her."

I close my eyes tightly. "It's ridiculous. It's been two

months and barely any time together. How can I *know* that?"

"When you know, you know. That's how I've always seen it," Victoria replies tenderly. "And besides, it sounds like she's decided to have your baby whether you're a part of it or not. That has to mean something."

"Yeah, like maybe she hates my guts."

Victoria tsks. "That's not what I meant. She's probably just as terrified as you are. An accidental pregnancy, her dad's best friend. I mean, that's a huge load. She doesn't know if she can trust you yet. What if she told you and you just walked away?"

"I'd never–"

"Yeah, *I* know that. But she doesn't." There's a glint in my sister's eye. "So, you have to tell her."

Before I can respond, the doorbell rings. Not even a moment later, there's a pounding at the door.

"Christ, who is that?" Victoria asks.

I get to my feet. "I don't know, but I have a guess."

I go to the front door; Victoria follows. "Grant, I don't want you to answer it. They sound mad."

I ignore her. I have to face the consequences of my actions. Especially because now I know I have no regrets.

When I open the door, I find exactly who I expected: Kent.

But I don't have a chance to greet him before he lunges toward me, growling, "You son of a bitch."

When we pull up to Grant's, the front door is hanging open and Dad's car is parked haphazardly in the driveway. Dana and I exchange a look.

"Well, this doesn't look *great*," Dana says softly.

I get out of the car and go up to the front door, half praying I'm not walking into a crime scene. I can hear Dad's voice, half-shouting from inside and then a woman's voice responding, calm, cool, and collected. Must be Victoria.

I walk inside and follow the voices into the living room. Grant is sitting in an armchair, head drooped back and a bag of frozen peas on his eye while Victoria calms down my dad, her hands on his shoulders while he massages a set of bruised knuckles on his right hand.

"What's going on?" I ask.

Everyone in the room looks at me in various states of distress.

Dad speaks first. "Harley, what are you doing here?"

"Trying to stop this from happening, but..." My eyes meet Grant's apologetically. "Evidently, I'm too late."

Grant gives me a lopsided smile. "Don't worry about it, Harley."

"Don't speak to her! Don't even look at–" my dad starts to yelp bullishly, trying to squirm away from Victoria.

"Dad! Stop it!" I cry out. "This is ridiculous!"

"Ridiculous?!" he says with incredulity.

"Kent, please...hear her out," Victoria murmurs, rubbing my dad's back.

I sigh. "I asked you not to punish Grant for my misgivings."

Dad looks away ashamed.

Grant sits up as best he can, reaching toward me. "Harley, this isn't all on you. I should have–"

"Please don't say you should have known better," I say ardently. "Please don't say you regret it."

He removes the bag of peas from his eye. The bruise is already forming deep purple around his eye socket.

"Because I..." I look to Dad and then to Dana who is just over my shoulder. *Deep breath.* "I don't."

Grant smiles, blue eyes twinkling with hope.

"I never wanted to hurt you, Daddy. But this is my life and the choices I make are mine. Grant and I...I can't explain it, but we have a connection. I haven't believed in the idea of love for a long time. Not since Mom left."

Dad's anger slips away, expression sorrowful and bereft.

"You weren't the only one blindsided," I say. "You know, I'm the reason you found out about Mom and Malcolm."

Dad frowns. "What are you talking about?"

"I was out in the treehouse that night during the Christmas party. I saw them go into the shed. And that's when I went in and told you I heard something funny outside, but..." I look down. "You went to go check it out and then everything fell apart. *I'm* the reason everything fell apart."

The room is silent. I've never even told my sisters this. It was always a sort of sad joke that I heard what sounded like a dying animal and it turned out to be the end of our parents' relationship.

But I knew what was going on. I just didn't have the heart to be the one to catch Mom in the act. "I couldn't let any of us live a lie anymore."

"I'm...well, I'm glad you did that. You've always been a brave girl," Dad says, trying to smile. "I'm just sorry you had to see that."

I shake my head. "It's not your fault. Nor is it your fault that since then I've never believed that love is real. I've tried to get around it my own way, but it's never stuck." I glance at Grant, feel my chest puff up with confidence. "Until now."

Grant doesn't break my gaze. Somehow, I know he's trying to tell me I'm not alone in this.

"Trust me, Daddy, I've seen you hurt before. I would never want to do that to you. But staying away from Grant is hurting *me*."

Dad looks away and sighs. "Is this how you feel too, Grant?"

"I haven't stopped thinking about Harley since the moment she answered the door at the Fourth of July party," Grant replies. But he looks right at me.

I smile.

"You didn't know about the baby, did you?" my dad asks him.

"Not until Dana mentioned it earlier," Grant chuckles nervously. "Still processing that one."

I chew on my lower lip. "Sorry."

"It's okay. It's...this is all complicated," Grants says in a voice made for me alone. If only I could go right over to him and take him up in my arms. I want to care for him so bad, talk about everything that's happened, figure out what's between us.

"God, I feel..." Dad starts to speak. "I feel so..."

Dana basically reads my mind. "Daddy, why don't the three of us go for a walk and leave the two of them alone for a bit to sort things out?"

He finally looks up, glancing at me and then at Grant. For a split second, I'm afraid he's going to grab me by the wrist at march me home. Instead, he nods slowly. "Alright."

Victoria walks Dad over to Dana. I try to look into my Dad's eyes, but he won't even look at me. "Daddy..."

"I just need some time, Harley," he says. "It's all coming at me so fast."

I give them a wide berth as they leave the living room and watch as they exit the house, the front door shutting behind them.

I feel Grant's hand on my shoulder. All the tension in my body fades away. I turn into his touch and throw my arms around him, burying myself in his chest. No more distance. Just closeness. *Real* closeness. Not the hidden kind.

Grant holds me close. "We have a lot to talk about."

"I know, just let me hold you." I squeeze him tighter. "Please."

He threads his fingers through my hair. "I've got you, Harley."

There is heat in my belly. Not arousal. Connection. Something about carrying this man's baby makes me want to be closer to him than ever. I tried to deny it for too long.

I know we don't have much time, so I finally draw

away from him, looking up into his eyes. "I'm sorry I didn't tell you about the baby, it was all just so complicated."

"It's alright. I...understand why you kept it from me." Grant touches my cheek. "I want to be there, Harley."

My heart gallops. "Of course, you can."

"But I'm..." His breath is short and shallow. "I'm scared."

Grant Neville? Scared? "Why?"

"Because what if I'm a terrible father?"

"You won't be," I reply, clinging to his waist. "I know you won't be."

Grant slips out of my grasp, scratching the back of his head. "You don't know that. You don't know for sure." He crosses away from me and then sighs. "Listen, I don't know how much you know about my past."

Not much, honestly. I know that he practically raised Victoria, although I don't know the reasons. To be frank, Grant was just my dad's friend all of my life. I didn't spend a lot of time caring to get to know him until now. Perhaps that makes me selfish, I just think I was young. Things were still waiting to align.

Now here we are.

"You can tell me as little or as much as you want, Grant." I carefully sit on one of the luxurious sofas. "I'll listen as long as you need."

Grant glances back at me, almost surprised. "Um. Alright. Well, I guess my situation was sort of like yours in that I watched the dissolution of my parents' love. Happened in the blink of an eye." He goes to lean on the mantle. "Although, unlike you, things weren't... picture-perfect up until then." He hesitates before continuing. "My parents were physically abusive to one another. It would either be like their love was the most beautiful thing in the world or the most dangerous."

"Oh, Grant, I'm so sorry."

"They never harmed me or Victoria. For some reason, there was a boundary there. But they had tunnel vision when it came to each other," he continues.

All the use of past tense verbs is giving me a sinking feeling in my stomach.

"They died in the middle of a physical altercation. It was the day of my graduation from high school and things were escalating. I tried to get them to stop and my mom pushed my dad." He drops his gaze to the floor. "He lost his footing, tripped into the street and there was an oncoming truck."

"Oh, my god..."

"And of course, she...tried to get to him before–" His voice breaks, but he shakes off the sorrow. "That's how I became Victoria's guardian."

I stare at Grant, wishing I could somehow alleviate the pain. I know as well as anyone, though, that the pain concerning our parents doesn't just go away. It somehow multiplies. Though my mother isn't dead, I've felt as though she is for a long time. Even being face-to-face with her didn't make her real. "Grant, I'm so sorry."

He clears his throat. "The point is, I'm not afraid that I'll be...abusive."

"No, of course not."

"But the intoxication, the tunnel vision. I don't want to lose myself in someone, and I don't want that for you either. You know, I'm older and you're probably not looking to slow down any time soon, so–"

"Well, I'm pregnant. I'm going to have to slow down for at least a little bit."

Grant pauses, taken a bit off-guard. He nods. "Yeah. That's true. A baby...*our* baby needs safety. Not the drama of a relationship. I don't know if I know what that looks like."

"You're thinking about it. I think that's a good sign already."

Grant smiles.

"Look, Grant, I've been with an older man before. It's why I left Australia."

"This is promising," he says sarcastically.

I giggle. "There's a point, I promise." I take a deep breath. "He was my professor. At the time."

"You're not a stranger to illicit affairs, then," he half-teases.

"No. Not at all." I laugh self-depreciatively. I shake my head. "I was young and I was blind. I was enchanted by the fact that he wanted me around all the time, always worried about if I was okay and wanting to know who I was with. It took me longer than I care to admit that he wasn't sweet and caring and loving. He wasn't a worried lover. He was a controlling jerk." My eyes drift away as so many memories flood through my mind. Moments I'd think fondly of him now painted in a whole new light.

" Paul, that was his name, by the way, wanted me to live in his golden cage. I was a pretty, young thing that he owned and controlled at will. A sort of trophy. A young woman with her whole life ahead of her that was under his spell and control. His thrall." I take a moment, breathing deeply. Reminding myself I'm no longer there.

"He consumed me. I was at his disposal almost constantly in all ways. At first, a few friends tried to warn me, but I was so in love with him, or so I thought, that I dismissed their worries, and little by little, they started being around less and less. It's okay, I thought, I don't need anyone else if I can just have him. And boy did I have him. Every second of my free time was to be spent with him or for him. Time went by and my life was classes, studying, and Paul, nothing else." I take a deep breath. "Then, one day I woke up and it dawned on me. Two years had gone by and I hadn't seen my family. I hardly ever talked to any of them for more than a minute or two at a time. That's when I realized what he had done to me. Keeping me from my own fucking life. So, I left."

Grant and I keep solid, steady eye contact.

"All that is to say, I'm stronger than I was then. Smarter. I wouldn't let you use me up like that."

"I wouldn't want you to."

I smile. "That's already a big difference between you and Paul."

Silence. Grant eyes me from across the room. "You really want to do this."

I nod. "I want to try. Don't you?"

Grant's brow bends. He takes a deep breath and then crosses to me. He sinks down onto his knees before me and wraps his arms around my waist. "Harley?"

"Yes, Grant?" I carefully push pieces of his dark hair out of his eyes.

"I want you."

I grin. "I want *you*."

"Not just for the baby. I want *you*. All of you. However you want to be."

"Same," I reply, cupping his cheeks in my hands. I carefully outline the rim of his bruised eye. He did that for me. "That's exactly how I want you, too."

"And it might be crazy, but I love you. I just know it."

I can't believe my ears. After all of this, Grant not only

wants to give things a shot between us, but he loves me? This is what I've been praying for every night without even realizing it. Dreaming of Grant at all hours of the day. This is my wildest dream come true. I kiss him and the fireworks go off.

"Does this mean you love me too?" he mutters into my mouth.

I laugh. "Yes, obviously."

"Say it, will you? Say it for me."

"Grant, I love you."

"Mm." He kisses me deeper. "God, one more time."

"Grant..."

"Yes...?" He leans closer to me, pushing me back onto the couch.

"I love you."

"Fuck, you don't know what that does to me."

I laugh. "Easy, you can't go full force on me like before."

"Of course, not." Grant slides his hand down my stomach. "Wouldn't dream of it."

I hope our baby has his gorgeous blue eyes. Maybe with my blonde hair. That would be just darling.

Grant kisses my stomach softly, nuzzling into my belly. "I'll be here every moment, Harley. Whatever you need. Whatever I can do." He lifts his head, eyes sparkling with tears. "You're having my baby."

"I am," I reply joyfully.

He kisses me again and runs his hands down my waist. "Let me take care of you. What do you need?"

"You," is the obvious answer. My body is aching for him. Has been ever since the Fourth of July. Now, though, the ache is deeper. Stronger. I have many, many ways for him to take care of me. "Want you inside," I whisper between hungry kisses.

Grant gasps for breath. "Is that okay?"

"Yes, more than. I need you."

"Oh god..."

Grant hooks his arms around me and pulls me off the couch, down onto the ground so I'm on top of him. I straddle his hips, still kissing him voraciously. He slides his hands around my bottom, pulling at the bike shorts.

"You don't know how much I need this," I say.

"Then let's get these off."

Grant shoves my shorts down while I undo the closure on his pants. "We don't have much time."

"Would only make things worse if he caught us–"

"Shhhh..." I drop my mouth to his ear. "Please don't talk about my dad when I'm about to fuck you."

"Oh, you're about to fuck me, are you?"

I laugh lowly. "Grant, I'm about to be the best you've ever had."

"As if you weren't alrea–" Grant is cut short when he feels my center slide against his hard, throbbing cock. "Oh my fucking god."

I undulate my hips back and forth slowly.

"Tell me you want me."

"So bad. I want you so...oh..." He nudges up against my center and I moan with him. "God, Grant, I want you so bad."

Grant slides his hand up to my lower back. "Use me, baby. Whatever you need, I'll give it to you."

I slide up until he is almost completely out and sink back down, my nerves flaring with desire. I relish the sound he makes, choking as he feels my tightness. I take him little by little until he's all the way inside. I have to wait a moment to enjoy the here and now. The man I love, who loves me, every inch of him inside me. Our baby still so small, ready to grow and be born into our life of love.

I'm committed to that last part. That's what it's going to be.

"You're so beautiful, Harley," Grant murmurs. His hands slide up my back and then down to my thighs. "You're glowing."

I laugh. "Am I?"

"Yes. Just radiant."

I sigh. For the first time in weeks, the world feels right.

Grant places his hands against my lower belly. "We belong to each other, Harley."

I put my hands against his. For some reason, a wave of intense arousal crashes over me. An almost biological passion. We've become as close as two people can be.

And it feels fucking amazing.

I start to roll my hips against his, warming with each stroke.

"There you go, good girl."

I keep his hands up against my lower belly, locking my fingers with his. "I don't think...I won't last..." I sigh. "Feels so fucking amazing."

"That's alright, baby, you do what you need to do. I want you to feel good."

I drop my head back as pleasure seeps through my veins. I work my hips faster, breath coming fast and hard. "Fuck, fuck." I can't keep from going at top speed, my whole body shaking. "I need–I need–"

Grant pulls me down onto his chest and takes the lead, his hips thrusting upward, pressing his length into me.

I scream into his neck in pleasure. "Yes, yes, yes."

"Take every inch, baby."

I cling to him.

"I feel you. You're close."

I can't speak, the heat in my pelvis growing to an inferno until I can no longer stand it. My body jerks as an orgasm rushes through me. I gasp for air. The euphoria is greater than anything I've ever felt. A combination of my sensitivity from pregnancy and my solidified connection with Grant.

"I've got you," he murmurs, "I...fuck."

My pussy clenches with pleasure, pushing Grant to come. He releases his full self inside. Not that we need it. He's already done the trick.

I still feel that rush of danger, the what-if feeling.

Grant kisses me and strokes the back of my head. "Is everything alright?" he asks, trying to maintain balance despite still basking in pleasure. "Are you okay?"

"Never better," I reply.

Grant grins. "That's how I like it."

I roll off him onto the floor, catching my breath. I can feel his eyes on me. And for the first time, it feels a hundred percent right.

"Harley."

I turn to look at him. "Grant."

"I love you."

I beam and giggle. "I love you."

"But I think I love you more."

"No, I'm having your baby, I definitely love you more."

We go back and forth like this as we get ourselves clothed and settled again, ready for the others to return. I may not be wound in his arms, but I just know now that I'm his, it would take a legion of soldiers to get me away.

I slip my arms around Harley, burying my face into her pillow-mussed hair. I can't get enough of her first thing in the morning. Breathing in her scent, loving her.

"Morning," she says groggily.

I kiss the back of her neck and slide one of my hands down to her midsection. "You're bigger today."

Harley laughs. "You're full of shit."

"No, I'm not," I say, tracing my thumb back and forth over her skin. "I swear, I can feel it." I get up onto my elbow and look into Harley's beautiful, languid eyes. "After all, I've been sleeping next to you for three weeks."

After Harley and I confessed our love for one another, we decided to try regular old dating. But given how fast things had already gone (hello, baby on the way), it was hard to keep apart. After a week of her sleeping over every night, she moved into my home in the hills.

It has been an adjustment, of course. I've never had to share my space with a lover. And Harley and I sort of bypassed all the logistical things in the name of passion and romance. Now, there's a bottle of oat milk in the fridge, another toothbrush on the sink, another person in my bed.

And I love all of it.

Of course, there is the matter of Kent. After he returned with Victoria and Dana, he made it clear he still needed time to process his feelings. It broke both Harley's and my hearts, but how could I begrudge him his emotions in this situation? He still speaks with Harley from time to time, but never to me. I miss my friend. But I'd rather the woman I love have her father.

I just don't know if I will be able to bear his distance for the rest of my life.

Harley's sisters, on the other hand, have embraced us as a couple with open arms. In fact, it feels like at least one of them is here every day. We've even babysat her niece Stella a couple of times. Brings me back to the days Victoria was little. Of course, then, I was just her older brother. Not her caregiver. It's going to be a whole different ballgame to raise a baby from birth.

Harley rubs my bicep, taking in a deep breath. "Well, congratulations. I'd say you're a really lucky man."

"Oh, I know. Trust me." I lean down and kiss her softly. Yes, the chemistry is off the fucking charts, but that doesn't mean we can't have tender soft moments. Doesn't always have to be tearing each other's clothes off. Although...I do love those moments too. "How are you feeling?"

"I was going to ask *you* that. Big day ahead."

I sigh. "Yeah, trying not to think about it."

"Grant..."

"Look, let me focus on you. I want to take care of you right now, not the other way around," I say, smoothing her hair out from her forehead.

"You know, the taking-care-of thing is a two-way street, babe."

I grin. "I love when you call me babe."

"God, are you like in love with me or something?" Harley says teasingly.

"Something like that."

Harley pecks my lips and then rolls out of bed. "I feel just peachy." She stretches her arms upward. Groaning with relief. "Now, you."

I collapse back into bed. "I'm fine."

"You're nervous."

"No shit I'm nervous."

Harley crosses her arms, smiling at me tenderly. "How can I help?"

I look up at the ceiling. Today, I'm seeing Malcolm in court. I know how it's going to go. I've done the work to make sure he doesn't get a lick of Infinium. I have a smoking gun that no judge will be able to ignore.

Still, having to face him, my old friend...someone I thought I'd get to grow old with and share memories with in the old folk's home. It's a bit of a mindfuck. Not to mention, I'm not sure if I've lost Kent too.

I might be totally friendless in this world.

"Hey." Harley comes to the side of the bed and leans over me.

It will have been worth it for Harley. I know it. "Yes?"

"You're Grant fucking Neville. And no one fucks with you," she murmurs and then kisses my forehead.

"You always say the most romantic things," I chuckle.

"Don't act like that didn't turn you on a little bit."

She knows me too well. "Oh, it did. It definitely did." I wrap my arms around her waist and yank her back into bed.

Harley laughs loudly, only cut off when I seal my lips to hers in a deep kiss.

"You know," she says, breathlessly pulling away. "I have a good idea about how to get rid of some of your nerves."

"Oh yeah?"

"Yeah..." Harley's hand sneaks below the covers toward my groin. "Can I show you?"

"Yes, please," I say with a sigh of pleasure.

Harley knows just the way to make me forget all my worries.

THE TRIAL so far has been going swimmingly. As this is a bench trial, the only person whose opinion matters is the judge. And so far, I think my lawyers are doing a great job of making our case.

"Exhibit C," Francis explains to the judge, pointing at the image on the screen. "This is the check that the plaintiff gave the defendant."

"Read it, please, counselor," the judge encourages.

"Pay to the order of Grant Neville the sum of fifty thousand dollars. Signed Malcolm Jenkins." Francis gestures to the bottom left corner of the image. "The memo reads, 'Don't go spending it all in one place,' with a written emoticon of a winking face."

Those in the gallery chuckle. Malcolm glares back at them. Behind him sits Aileen. She looks as elegant as ever, skin pulled taut from who knows how many cosmetic surgeries. Her upkeep must be quite expensive.

The judge hits his gavel. "Order, order." But I can see a hint of a smirk on his lips.

"In all seriousness, Your Honor, this suggests that this

gift, while enormous, was one of friendly generosity. There is nothing that suggests this money must be utilized for the plaintiff's own capital gain."

Malcolm rustles in his seat. He looks less like an honorable businessman and more like a kid who should probably run to use the bathroom.

Francis continues to explain the exhibits we've presented to the court including email communications I shared with Malcolm after he gifted me the money. The friendliness and lack of gravity in the exchanges only support my case that this was a gift. Not an investment.

When it comes time for witness testimony, Malcolm's lawyers call me, for some godforsaken reason, Aileen, and then Malcolm. I am cordial with the lawyer examining me but don't have much to offer him.

It isn't until Malcolm's cross-examination that things get interesting.

"Mr. Jenkins, can you attest that you wrote this check?" Francis asks, holding up the baggie containing the original check. Thank god I've kept such detailed records over the years.

Sour-faced Malcolm shrugs. "I don't know. I write a lot of checks."

"Can you at least say this is your signature?"

"It looks like my signature, but it wouldn't be the first time someone has used it for their own personal gain."

I clutch the arms of my chair, restraining myself from making an angry grunt. This is ridiculous. This petulant fuckhead is going to do whatever he can to get his way. Until the very last second, I'm sure.

"Lucky for you, we have a side-by-side comparison. Maybe this will help you jog your memory." Francis points up to the screen. "This was your signature on the court documents from this morning. And this is your signature from the check. Would you say this is your signature, Mr. Jenkins?"

As the court waits for his answer, I'm distracted by the sound of a door squeaking open. I turn around and am shocked when my eyes land on Kent Solace standing at the back of the gallery. He's trying to sneak in quietly and clearly didn't anticipate the door betraying his covertness. "Sorry," I see him mouth to the bailiff near the door. He slips into the back row, and just before he sits, his eyes meet mine. I'd wave if I could. In fact, I'd run to him and give him a great big bear hug. I had no idea he was coming, but there is no doubt in my mind, he's here to support me.

It must have taken a lot to put everything aside to be here.

"Yes, that's my signature, I guess," Malcolm finally says gruffly with a roll of his eyes.

"Thank you, Mr. Jenkins. No further questions."

I don't even care about the case anymore. Okay, that's not entirely true. For the first time, though, I feel like I could lose and be alright. Because Kent is trying to send me a message. He's here for me. He may not like me. He might still want to punch me in the face. And that would all be valid. But he's still here for me.

That's all I can ask for.

Fortunately, I don't have to pick and choose. The judge has a ruling quickly after closing arguments. "The defendant is not liable for claims the plaintiff has made."

"Not liable" are the only two words I need. I'm free. Free from this fucked up run around Malcolm has put me through. My lawyers and I stand, shaking hands, sighing with relief. Inside, I feel like I'm on top of the world. I've kept my company, Kent is back, and Harley will be home waiting for me.

Maybe I'm doing *something* right.

I turn and find Kent standing now at the front of the gallery, reaching for me. "Congratulations."

I take Kent's hand and shake it heartily. "Thank you." I can't help myself. I pull him into a hug. He doesn't resist, clapping me on the back. We have a lot to work through, but I know this is a sign that we're both committed to it. We don't just owe it to Harley. We owe it to each other. "Thank you for being here."

We break apart and lock eyes. "I'm just sorry I was late," Kent says with a half-smile. "I had meetings and then it was...well..." He glances over at Aileen who is engaged in a tense, quiet argument with Malcolm.

"I know you put a lot aside to be here."

Kent sighs and shakes his head.

"Go talk to them," I encourage.

Kent's eyes widen. "What?"

"Just...they're right there. Go add insult to injury," I reply.

"I couldn't, that wouldn't be–"

"Kent, there are things you never got a chance to say to them. You owe it to yourself."

Kent lifts his head, considering my words. "Alright. Would you come with me?"

"Of course."

Kent and I cross to the other side of the gallery. When Malcolm and Aileen realize we're coming, they shoot daggers at us, immediately sidling up together. A united front. Kent opens his mouth to speak but isn't able to get out more than, "Hi."

"This isn't the best time, Kent," Aileen says snootily.

"I'd like to respect that, Aileen, but I'm afraid I don't feel compelled to do that after you disrespected so much of my time when we were married," Kent replies with venom I've never heard from him.

I seal my lips together. He's got this covered.

Aileen opens her mouth in shock. Malcolm picks up where she left off. "You may not speak to her like that."

"You're right, I should save my anger for you, shouldn't I, old *friend?*" Kent answers, voice bouncing with laughter. "I just came over to give you my condolences regarding the case and–" He lasers in on Aileen. "I don't know if this needs saying, considering I'm sure you'll be leaving town as soon as your husband's business is all finished up, but just in case..." Kent looks like a falcon in the dive, ready to snap up his prey with ease. I haven't seen this strength in him in decades, if ever. At least not in the past ten years for sure. "You are *not* welcome in my home anymore. And you are *not* welcome near my children."

The word "my" hits Aileen squarely between the eyes.

"*Your* children?"

Kent smiles solemnly. "Come on, Aileen. You don't have to pretend you care any longer." He takes a step away from the insidious duo, holding up his hands. "You are absolved. Best of luck with everything."

Aileen lets out a furious growl. It's funny to watch her pout and fume.

"Well, I'd say it's been a pleasure doing business with you, but..." I trail off, looking at Malcolm. "Safe travels."

"You'll fucking pay one day, Grant. Mark my words."

"Oh, Malcolm, stop pretending like you're a Bond villain. You're just a regular guy, and a quite pitiful one at that," I say with a haughty laugh and then follow Kent through the gallery and out of the courtroom.

He has his hand pressed to his heart. "I did it."

I put my arm around his shoulder and shake him. "Fuck yeah, you did. You *eviscerated* them."

"Oh god, was I mean?" Kent asks with puppyish eyes. "I don't know half of what I said, I just said it."

I smile at my friend. "Come on. Let me buy you a drink."

Kent and I take a drive to one of our old haunts back in the day, a cash-only Irish pub with heady beer and sticky floors. We manage to avoid talking about the elephant in the room until we're both half a Guinness deep. That's when Kent sighs; I know that sigh. The sigh of "We have something we have to talk about".

"You ready?" I ask with a nervous smile.

"As I'll ever be," Kent says. "I mean…" He looks down into the foam of his beer. "Look, three weeks down and I'm already afraid of what I'll miss out on by keeping you at arm's length."

"You still see Harley…"

"Sure, but it's not the same. I guess it won't ever be. But I know it will feel better not trying to talk around the fact that she loves you. That she's chosen you." Kent lifts his brown eyes to meet mine. "Man, this is weird."

I nod. "I know. It's not a situation I ever imagined we'd be in, believe me."

"That's good to know," Kent laughs awkwardly. "I can tell she's really happy. The pregnancy was really draining her before you came into the picture and…I know that she's strong enough to do it alone and she would do it that way if she wanted. But it's clear you're good for her."

"You have no idea how happy that makes me, Kent."

Kent smiles. "And, as weird as it is, I'm happy for you. You're in love, you're going to be a dad. I'm happy to see you finally settling down with someone...even if it is my daughter."

"Me too. I never imagined it'd be possible."

"Me either."

We both laugh. "Harley's special. I know you don't need *me* to tell you that. But I feel so lucky that she's chosen me."

Kent takes a swig of beer. "You are a lucky bastard, Grant. I could've cold-cocked you again and you would have deserved it."

"Not going to argue with that."

"Still weird, but as long as you promise me to always do right by my daughter, I think I can get past it."

I consider my old friend. Thirty years of friendship is nothing to sniff at. We've been through a lot together. More than a lot. We're practically brothers. "You have my word, Kent."

Kent nods and then holds up his beer. "To Harley."

"To Harley," I reply.

We clink our glasses together. And I know as long as I live, I'll make good on my promise. In just a few short months, Harley has become my whole world.

Today might have been about fighting for Infinium. But from this day on, my mission has completely shifted. Making a beautiful life with Harley and our child will be my life's greatest work.

No one can stop me.

THE FIRST THING I notice when I get home is the overwhelming aroma of garlic and onions, aka delicious.

"Harley?" I call out. I peek into the kitchen. It's an absolute mess in there, like a tornado went through it. But no Harley to be seen. I frown and stroll into the dining room. "Harley, where are you?"

In the distance, I can hear music. Sounds almost like it's...outside.

I walk through the house and onto the terrace, which takes longer than you'd expect, and find Harley standing at a table set for two. She's wearing a darling little dress covered with an apron that is covered in red splotches, more like a butcher than a chef. However, given that the meal is spaghetti, I'll have to chalk up the stains to tomato sauce.

"What's all this?" I ask, holding my arms open in joyful surprise.

Harley grins and rushes over to me, taking off the apron and tossing it on the ground before leaping into my arms and kissing me right on the lips. "Welcome home," she murmurs.

I kiss her again, her lips as sweet as candy. "I feel like I should try my entrance again since you're dressed up like Lucille Ball."

"You're showing your age, babe." Harley giggles. She takes my hand and guides me over to the table. "Are you hungry?"

"Starving...but what's the occasion?"

Harley scoffs, "You won your case!"

Of course, the case. "Funnily enough, that was the least important thing that happened today."

She pulls out a chair for me and pats it. "Tell me all about it."

Over a spaghetti dinner, I share with her the events of the day, including what happened between me and her father. Harley smiles the whole time, happy beyond compare. "I told him he should go to the trial, actually," she says, spiraling spaghetti onto her fork.

"Oh?"

"Well, he asked me if he should. I think he was a little nervous to see Mom, but..." Harley reaches out and takes my hand. "I told him how much it would mean to you and to me."

I hum thoughtfully. "To us."

"Yes, although I didn't say that. I think the concept of 'us' is still cringeworthy to my dad," she says with a shrug. "I'm just glad he decided to go."

I consider Harley, the woman I love, for a brief moment. Her crop of blonde hair hangs in waves, framing her face. Her eyes are warm and safe. I'm excited to call them home for the rest of my life.

"Me too. Thank you for encouraging him."

"Of course. The last thing I ever wanted was to get between you two. You know that."

"I felt the same way."

"Biology had other things in mind, I guess," Harley says with a shy smile, leaning back in her chair and touching her stomach.

I beam proudly. "Not just biology..." I get up from the chair and hold my hand out to her.

Harley takes it hesitantly. "What are you doing?"

I guide her up from her seat and pull her into my arms, the music that's been a backing track to our meal swooning in the background. "Dance with me."

Harley laughs, head hanging back, clinging to me as I sway her side to side. "I never knew you were such a romantic, Grant."

"Honestly, me either. Guess you just bring it out of me."

We find our footing and our rhythm, something we are

much better at horizontally, and dance as a soulful singer croons, seemingly only for us. Though the stars light up the night sky above us, the only stars I see are Harley's fiery eyes. I lower my mouth to her ear and whisper, "I can't wait to have a baby with you, Harley."

She turns her face into my cheek and sighs contentedly. "You're lucky you don't have to wait very long, then."

If you had asked me six months ago what my life would look like now, I'd probably just say, "More of the same." Business as usual. Developing projects, putting out fires, making more money than I know what to do with.

My whole life in just three months has changed. Not just because I have a beautiful woman in my arms committed to starting a family with me. But also because I believe in love. I don't know if I ever did, even as a child.

Now, though, I believe in love so wholeheartedly that I know it should scare me.

Yet, with Harley, it doesn't.

I kiss the side of her head and breathe in her scent.

We stop our lackadaisical dancing and embrace tightly under the night sky. I can't wait for thousands more nights like this with her. The rest of my life if I play my cards right.

"Grant," she whispers, fingers digging into my back.

"What, my love?"

She pulls back, looking into my eyes. "I've needed you all day."

My lips part. I know what she means. More than my presence, more than my stories from the day. She needs my body. My attention.

I would never deny my woman that need.

"I'm here now," I murmur and start a trail of kisses down from her temple to her jaw. "What can I do for you?"

She bends her neck to the side giving me more room to kiss her neck. "Take me up to our bed, Grant."

Our bed. Just a few weeks and what was once mine is now ours. Some men committed to bachelordom might shudder at the thought. Not me. Not for one second.

"Take me to our bed and make love to me."

I groan into her neck, sliding my hands down her back to her waist.

"Please."

"You don't have to beg, Harley." I lift her into my arms, bridal style. She laughs, wrapping her arms around my neck. "I'll do whatever you say."

She dangles her legs back and forth, resting her head on my shoulder. "How did I get so lucky?"

"You know it's me who should be asking you that."

I carry her into the house, over the threshold. My heart flutters with the hope that someday, someday soon, I'll be able to carry her into our house like this on the day of our wedding. We've yet to discuss the subject of marriage. But given how we've been failing to take one thing at a time, I wouldn't be surprised if that comes sooner rather than later.

Ignoring all the mess of the day, I carry her up the stairs, my strength not faltering for a minute, and take her into our room. The massive king bed is perfectly made, the white comforter the perfect place for me to lay Harley down and admire her lithe form in the sheets.

"Mm, won't you join me?" she asks, stretching her body out long.

"Of course, but first I want to admire you."

Harley smiles, her eyelids low. Tempting me. "You like what you see?"

"Oh, Harley, you know my answer to that."

She closes her eyes and giggles. "Love."

I was afraid at first that she would be too young for me. But any woman, no matter their age, can act girlish. If anything, it makes me want to remember what it felt like to be a boy. After all, that's what we are at our base parts, just a girl and a boy who have fallen deep into one another. "Yes. Love what I see."

I unclasp my belt and throw it to the side. Then, my pants. We don't need to hurry anymore. We can take our time. And while the thrall of tearing each other's clothes off is satisfying, sometimes, I like to keep things simpler. Purer, almost.

Harley follows my cue and pulls her dress over her head, revealing her beautiful, braless breasts. They've already grown bigger in preparation for our baby.

For now, though, all we can do is enjoy them.

"God, you're stunning," I say.

Harley bites her lower lip and then works her panties down her legs, leaving her naked in my bed. She's like Aphrodite being born of the bounteous sea. A work of art. Right there. All for me. "Get naked and come lie with me."

"Yes, ma'am." I pull off my shirt and briefs, ignoring how hard I've gotten, and crawl into the bed next to her.

"Hold me."

I wrap my arms around her and pull her into my arms, her ass flush against my erection. I'm not in any hurry. In fact, I don't even have to fuck her. Just her body next to mine is enough.

Harley sighs as if she has something to say but remains silent.

"What is it, darling?" I ask.

She is quiet. Her moods are something I have noticed more since learning she's pregnant. They are not so much swinging as they are sudden. And quiet. I am still learning how to work them out of her. I don't want her to worry about scaring me away or trying to keep me.

I kiss her shoulder. "I'm here."

Harley takes my hand in hers, our fingers interlacing, and presses it to her belly. "I think you're right. I am bigger today."

"You sound sad about that."

"I'm not sad, I'm just..." She twists her head back to look at me. "I'm just going to get bigger, Grant."

"Is that what happens when you're pregnant? I never knew that," I tease.

She attempts to laugh, but the tail end falls off with despondency. "What if you're not attracted to me anymore?"

"Harley–"

"We haven't even made it a month. What if you suddenly think I'm disgusting or–"

"Harley, listen to me." I can't let her finish. There's no way I'm going to let her spiral out of control when I know what's true. I touch her cheek softly. "You're having my baby, Harley."

Her brown eyes are watering. No tears. Not when things are so wonderful.

"I can't wait to see your body change..." I pull our clasped hands up to my mouth and kiss her knuckles. "And grow. And do everything it's meant to. All because you've given me this gift."

"Really?"

I smile at her tenderly. "How can I prove it to you?" I drop my hand back to her stomach. I wasn't lying this morning. I can tell things are starting to change. I'm sure she'll pop before we know it. And that thought stirs something in me that I'm too shy to explain. I slide my hand a bit lower, finding the apex of her pussy. "Hm?"

Harley's eyes flutter shut as I daintily prod her clit. "Oh, Grant..."

"I'm going to be here every step of the way," I whisper, dipping my fingers into her. "I'm here for whatever you need. *Whatever*. I mean it."

She grabs onto my bicep and moans. "So good..."

"You're the love of my life, Harley. You're my woman."

"Yes, yes, I'm–" I pinch her clit and she squeals.

"You're so sensitive," I laugh lowly.

She pulls on my arm. "Inside me. Inside me now."

I try to keep foreplay long, but she's so needy for my cock that I can't refuse her. I get up on my knees and part her legs. "You don't have to do a thing, Harley." I place the head of my cock at her entrance. The image of our parts anticipating one another is so fucking beautiful. "Just let me take care of you."

Harley nods into the bed, her mouth lolling open. Poor thing. So needy.

I push myself forward, slipping deeper inside. Harley gasps, her leg bending against my chest. I feel fucking amazing, but her pleasure is always paramount to mine. "Are you alright?"

"More than, Grant."

I put my hand on her hip and begin to slide in and out of her. "You feel fucking amazing."

She laughs. "You always say that."

"Is that a problem?" I tease and then fuck her faster.

Harley wasn't ready for that. She yelps in pleasure and grabs one of the pillows. "Fuck! Oh my god, fuck."

I slow down. "Sorry, just can't get enough of you."

She eyes me over her shoulder and shakes her head. "I fucking hate you."

We both smile. Thank goodness hate and love are not opposites. "You comfortable?"

"Uh-huh," she nods, pulling the pillow closer. "Keep going."

I drive my cock in and out of her, increasing my speed incrementally, not all at once. I watch as Harley's body unfurls, all the tension built up from missing me throughout the day disappearing into the ether. Each of my thrusts is met with a whine from her. Music to my ears.

Meanwhile, my arousal only grows. Her pussy is soft, luscious, and tight. A perfect home for my cock. I've learned over the years how to last long for a woman, but Harley challenges me. I have to be careful or else I might just lose it all at once.

"You need my cock, baby?" I ask.

"Yes, I need your–" Harley's eyes roll back. "Fuck, you feel so good."

God, what an image. I clench my teeth and pound harder. "You want it, baby?"

"Yes, I need it. Give it to me." Harley grips the pillow tighter and pushes her face into it, letting out a primal scream of pleasure.

"Fuck, yes. Take it, baby. Take it." My hips are working without me, completely out of my control. All I can do is let it happen, admire her beautiful body. Imagine how it will grow with my seed.

Fuck, it just drives me wild.

"I have to come, I have to–" she moans. Euphoria washes over her, her body jerking and head snapping back as the orgasm overcomes her. "Grant, please, please, please..."

I can't do anything else but ride out her orgasm with her, which isn't hard, considering how her pussy grips me, pulling me deeper. "Fuck, I'm coming too, I'm..."

"Do it. Do it, baby."

I force my hips forward with a final smack and burst inside. I gasp, gripping her hips, my fingers indenting her skin deeply. I'm at a loss for words, brain numb with pleasure until I finally can catch my breath. "Oh my fucking, *god*, baby..." I mutter. "Holy shit."

Harley reaches for me. "Come here," she whispers. "Come to me."

I collapse into her arms and curl around her body, pressing my face against her chest.

"Thank you," she says. "Thank you so much."

I kiss her sternum. "Of course, any time."

Harley laughs. "How did I get so lucky?"

I stroke her waist. Our little one, still incredibly little, will be big before we know it. It won't be just Harley and me. It will be the three of us. It's an intimidating thought, but without knowing it, I've prepared for this my whole life.

"It wasn't luck, Harley," I murmur. "Serendipity, maybe. The party was the universe bringing us together at the right time for both of us, I'm sure of it. But I think we've been working our whole lives to find each other."

Harley runs her hands through my dark hair and kisses my forehead. "You know what? I think you're right."

TWENTY-NINE
HARLEY

Four months later...

My sisters have gone to the trouble of renting out the coffee shop near Dad's place for a humble baby shower. I said I didn't want anything too fancy and, given my intense love for coffee cake since I fell pregnant, they thought there was no better place than the coffee shop that makes the best in Burbank.

They know me so well.

"Okay, finish up your guesses," Amy announces, shaking a bowl full of folded slips of paper.

"Do we really need to do this?" I ask for the fiftieth time. I told them no games, but Amy insisted that we all had to guess if the baby would be a Pisces or an Aries.

"It's important," she says with an air of pretension. "We need to be prepared for either scenario."

Kira sighs. "Amy, you know that astrology isn't a real science."

"Mm, said like a quintessential Cancer," Amy says.

"Yeah, and you're acting like a real *Leo* right now," Gillian teases.

Amy gapes. "I am not!"

"Of course you are! Stealing the scene at Harley's baby shower," Gillian continues.

I laugh as I watch the argument unfold, resting my hands on the top of my bump. At seven months pregnant, I'm starting to feel *big*. It's a nice feeling, although according to Gillian, I shouldn't get too comfortable. "The last month is going to be a slog, let me tell you," she explained to me. "And if you carry like me, you're going to be carrying late. Stella *was* nearly two weeks behind schedule, after all."

"I love you all, but I'm very glad I don't have sisters," Lola announces.

"I second that," Victoria adds with a grin in my direction. The two of us have become very close the past few months and she's even taken to calling me her "sister from another mister". Of course, chosen family is a lot different of a ballgame, but I'm grateful to have such a good relationship with Grant's sister. She doesn't yet know it, but we're going to ask her to be the godmother.

"Could you two quit it?" Dana asks, interrupting the feud.

"Yeah, tell me if my daughter's going to be a Pisces or an Aries!" I call out, shifting in my seat.

Amy clears her throat and tosses her hair over her shoulders. "Fine."

As she reads out the guesses, I start to feel my baby elbowing at my palm. She's getting way more active lately and I love every second of it. The rest of the world completely fades away when she starts to flit around.

"It's a tie!" Amy announces despondently. "Three to three!"

"Maybe she'll be a cusp," Lola reasons.

My little sister glares. "You still have to land on one side of the cusp."

"Stella, what do you think it's going to be?"

Stella pops her head up, her little blonde buns jumping. "What's the question?" Gillian brought along Stella at my request. I thought it would be a nice thing to share with her as her time as the only child of the Solace sisters comes to a close. She has been much less interested in the baby shower activities than her coloring book, though.

"Do you think your cousin is going to be a Pisces or an Aries? Pisces is a fish and Aries is a ram," Amy explains.

Stella's face sours. "I don't want Aunt Harley's baby to be a fish or a ram."

"There we go!" I announce. "The most sensible of us all."

"Amy, why don't you focus on taking some pictures and send a couple to Dad, alright?" Dana asks, smoothing her hands down Amy's shoulders.

Amy sniffs. "Fine."

I laugh and shake my head. My little girl is going to be born into a family of drama queens, that's for sure.

Dana walks off with Amy inevitably to talk her down from her disappointment the game didn't go to her liking. The rest of us start to chat idly until Lola pulls her phone out of her purse and sighs.

"Lola..." Gillian says warningly.

"Sorry, I'm sorry! Just my phone is blowing *up*." Lola tosses it back into her purse.

"Good things, I hope," Victoria says. "Maybe a man?"

Lola chuckles, "Yeah, a man, but not the kind you want to be blowing up your phone." She purposefully avoids looking at Gillian. "Just my brother."

"Ugh! What does he want?" Gillian snaps. "He knows you're busy, doesn't he?"

"Gill, relax, you know how he gets when he's stressed."

"What in the world does he have to be stressed about?" Gillian asks with a roll of her eyes.

Lola hesitates, looking askance at me. I know that look. After all, I've known Lola my whole life. Gillian and Lola have been thick as thieves since diapers. And that look means she knows what she's about to say is going to upset Gillian...and upsetting Gillian means things are about to go off the rails. "How about we–" I attempt to modulate the tone of the conversation.

"Harley, please," Gillian says. "Just tell me, Lola."

Her friend sighs. "He's looking at buying the lot by Seton."

Gillian's eyes widen with an ire I would not want to be on the other side of. I have definitely crossed her a few times in my life, but ever since I got pregnant, we've been closer than we've ever been. I am determined not to let her anger be directed at me ever again. "What?!"

"What's the lot by Seton?" Victoria asks.

I wince. She's just opened a can of worms.

"It's an abandoned lot by the school Stella goes to."

"How can you say that?! It's a playlot! Kids have birthday parties there."

"It's not recognized as that by the city, Gillian," Lola says uneasily.

Gillian shakes her head. "So what?! It's used by the community, it should be used for the community. Not whatever development project Axel is working on. We don't need more condos in California!"

Victoria looks at me. "Sorry, Harley."

I laugh and lean back. "No apologies necessary. I love the drama."

Kira has remained silent this whole time, but I feel her glare. That's enough to shut me up.

"Did you even try to explain to him—"

"You know I don't have a leg to stand on when it comes to Axel and his developments. He's a businessman!"

"Yes, he's a businessman. He doesn't care about anyone else but himself."

"Gillian, that's not fair!" Lola cries out.

Gillian tries to respond, but her anger is making her words come out strained and stilted. "I'm so *sick* of him!"

"Are you okay, Mommy?" Stella asks.

Gillian straightens up and takes a deep breath. "I'm fine, sweetie. I'm fine." She leans in toward the rest of us and lowers her voice. "I'm sorry, Lola. I'm just sick of him always popping up where he doesn't belong."

"For being so sick of him, you sure talk about him a lot," I say pointedly.

"I don't like what you're implying," Lola says, queasily grabbing her stomach.

"I'm just saying! With the way Gillian reacts like the sky is falling every time he does something that remotely relates to her, I'd say she's got a bit of a crush."

Victoria covers her mouth to hide a laugh.

Gillian lifts her chin and narrows her eyes. "I will hold my tongue because this is your baby shower, Harley."

I grin, "Thanks, sis."

We hear the door to the café open, a ringing bell quite literally saving my hide.

Dana and Amy reemerge from their conversation, Dana ready to take charge of kicking out this misguided patron.

"Oh, sorry, this is a private..." She gasps. "Grant! What are you doing here?"

I peek around her. Sure enough, there's Grant. "Honey, I told you to wait in the car."

Grant looks at me with his easy smile. "Ha, ha, very funny."

"This is a girls-only event, you know that," Victoria admonishes.

He runs his hand back through his dark hair, silver threads of hair shining. "Right. Yes, I do know that."

Something is off. I know it. We've been together such a short time, but it's been a lot in a very short time. His tells are as clear as day to me. When something is brewing under the surface, he keeps playing with his hair and smoothing out the front of his shirt. "What's going on?"

Grant swallows and rolls his eyes. "Well, I'd say 'nothing' but that would sort of defeat the purpose of why I'm here."

I frown, glancing around the room. Everyone is at a loss for words, except Amy, who snaps a photo on her phone. "Gotta capture every moment," she says to no one in particular.

"Could you stand, Harley?" Grant asks.

I put my hands on my belly and sigh. "Do I have to?"

The corner of Grant's smile jumps in exasperation. The sooner I follow his instructions, the sooner I get answers. "Help me up," I say to Kira.

She gives me her hand and I push myself up out of the chair.

"Okay, I'm up," I say through a laugh.

Grant looks at everyone. "Well, this is more intimidating than I thought it was going to be."

"Grant..." Dana says. "What are you doing?"

"I can't wait."

Her eyes widen. "So, you're doing it *now?*"

"Doing *what* now?" I ask in confusion.

"You're so impatient," Victoria scolds Grant. "You couldn't wait like five hours?"

"You try sitting on your hands at home waiting for something like this and then we'll talk," Grant replies quickly.

"Would someone tell me what's going on?!" I call out.

The room is once again silent. As I scan everyone's faces, I can just tell they know something I don't. Then, my eyes land on Grant. "Grant, just...what's this about?"

He takes a deep breath, his shoulders heaving. "I was going to wait until tonight. When you came home...but I just can't wait anymore, Harley."

"Okay?" I can't comprehend what he's doing at first, sinking down toward the floor. But once he's there, on bended knee, it all snaps into place. "Oh, my god..."

"Harley Elaine Solace."

"You're doing this? You're actually doing this? Right now?"

"*Apparently*, right now," Victoria grumbles.

Grant smiles. "Yes. Is that alright?"

I put my hand to my mouth and nod. Astonished.

"Our love story is unconventional. But I think it's one of the most beautiful ones that has ever been told. And there's only one thing that is left to do to make it complete." He opens the box, revealing a gorgeous ruby ring set amongst the most brilliant diamonds I've ever seen.

Tears start to swim in my eyes. This doesn't feel real.

"You filled a hole in my heart I never knew existed. You made me believe in love. You make me better every day," he says in a near whisper. Emotion is close to overcoming him.

There's a flurry of movement in my stomach. It's incredible how she can tell that what's happening just out of her reach is cause for celebration.

"Will you marry me?"

I nod. "Yes, of course. Of course, I'll marry you!"

Grant gets to his feet in an instant and pulls me into his arms. As soon as his lips touch mine, tears burst from my eyes. I can't help it. I never thought I'd have a love like this, let alone a whole baby and a marriage ahead of me.

When we break apart, Grant presses his forehead to mine. "I'm sorry I couldn't wait."

"It's okay. This was perfect. Better than perfect."

"I got it all on tape!" Amy squeaks excitedly.

I throw my head back in laughter. How could anything be better than sharing this moment with the women I love most in this world?

Grant takes my hand and slips the ring on. "Perfect fit, huh?" he says with a lopsided grin.

I know he's talking about the ring, but I feel like he's talking about us. I cup his cheek, relishing the prickle of his beard. "Yeah. Just perfect."

"Can I see?" Stella peeps at my side.

"Stella—" Gillian starts to pull her away.

"It's fine. Here, look, honey." I hold my hand out to her. "Isn't it pretty?"

Stella's eyes go wide. "Whoa. It's so sparkly."

Grant chuckles and wraps his arm around my waist. He's loved how I have filled out in pregnancy and can't take his hands off me most of the time. His hand spreads out against the side of my bump and he smiles proudly at me. I put my hand over his.

"Were you surprised?" he asked.

"Yeah, how could you tell?" I say sarcastically.

"Well, I guess this means we will have to have another baby shower since you ruined this one," Amy says through happy tears.

"Oh, absolutely," Grant replies. "It's only fair."

There's no way I'm letting Grant leave now that he's here, so he sits down with the rest of us, indulging in pastries and coffee, gabbing and laughing just like he's one of the girls. We call up Dad and have him come down to celebrate too. They've come a long way since everything fell out, hugging tightly when Grant tells him the news.

Dad and Grant sit on either side of me. Dad touches the nape of my neck and leans in to kiss me on the cheek. "Congratulations, Harley."

"Thank you, Daddy," I say.

He's got tears in his eyes when he draws away but won't look at me. They're not up for discussion. I reach out and grab his hand, holding it tightly. With my other hand, I grab Grant's hand. My cheeks hurt so bad from smiling, but I can't help it.

My life is so beautiful. Everyone in this room chose to be here. Chose me. Despite betrayal, anger, or hurt, we are all here together celebrating my baby, the product of love between Grant and me.

And I will choose all of them until my dying day. Through thick or thin.

That's just how we, Solaces, are.

www.ingramcontent.com/pod-product-compliance
Lightning Source LLC
Chambersburg PA
CBHW021348150726

47989CB00005B/2150